Amarias Adventures

Escape from Riddler's Pass

Amy Green

Published by Warner Press Inc, Anderson, IN 46012
Warner Press and "WP" logo is a trademark of Warner Press Inc.

ISBN: 978-1-59317-433-0

Editors: Robin Fogle, Karen Rhodes
Cover by Curtis D. Corzine
Design and layout: Curtis D. Corzine

Printed in the USA

To Jarod,

for being my brother
and my friend.

CHAPTER I

Looking down on the forest outside of Mir, Demetri did not see any ghosts among the trees.

Some crazy merchant, a fellow traveler on the mountain road, had sworn that ghosts—he called them *saards*—had been spotted in the area. "Just a few weeks past, one stood up on the bridge past this valley and shot five Patrol members with its blood-red arrows, then disappeared," he said solemnly. "None of the Patrol escaped alive."

"If none escaped, how do you know this *saard* stood on the bridge?" Demetri had pointed out.

The merchant had ignored him and continued, "I'm telling you, it's not safe to go into those woods, th-they're haunted."

That was why Demetri now sat on a boulder at the pass instead of on the mossy forest floor just a few dozen paces away. The merchant had insisted that he go no farther, and Demetri hardly wanted to call attention to himself by refusing. Besides, the sun was starting to sink in the sky. Ghosts or not, no one but thieves and lawbreakers moved about after curfew.

Of course, Demetri didn't believe the merchant's tale was anything more than local superstition. He remembered talk of *saards* when he had lived in District One long ago. *There is no truth to such wild stories.* Demetri was a Patrol captain and a Guard Rider, a man of reason who would not be swayed by legends.

Still, Demetri decided to set up camp in the pass outside the forest. He had put in many long days to reach Mir, often on little sleep, battling windstorms and, once, a group of bandits. He knew the three young people, hardly more than children, the ones he had been ordered to find and kill, would not be able to travel as quickly. They were Youth Guard—strong, determined, and quick-witted, but he was a hardened soldier, used to the conditions of the desert.

He had not carried a tent with him; the weight would have slowed him down, and the ground made a fine-enough bed. He had not slept well on his journey through the mountains, but that had been true since he had met Aleric and received his commission: kill the squad of Youth Guard who came through his town.

And I will, he vowed, fingering the Guard Rider medallion that hung beneath his shirt. *They escaped me in Da'armos, but this time that old desert fox, Samariyosin, won't be here to save them.*

Smugglers. Demetri had hated them, even back when he was an ordinary Patrol captain, and Samariyosin was one of the most notorious smugglers of all, even in his old age. It was Samariyosin's fault the three young people had escaped him. *But they will not escape this time.*

Demetri dug through his supplies and found a slice of stale bread. It was all he needed for supper. He was not hungry.

As he ate, he reviewed the strategy he had carefully planned late into the previous night before falling asleep.

One of the Youth Guard members was in Mir, sick from some sort of poison. The young crippled boy, the one who was not of the Guard at all, had told him that much.

In the morning, he would gather a detachment of Patrol members from Mir and the nearby villages. Together, they would search for the Youth Guard member—house to house if necessary. Once he killed the missing Guard member, he would wait. Wait for the others to come and join their friend.

He knew they would come. They seemed loyal. Too loyal. It was their weakness, and it would destroy them.

All of Demetri's fellow travelers were beginning to settle down for the night, feeding mules, putting up tents, and cooking supper over fires. Merchants and traders, mostly, though Demetri spied one small family in a dirty, broken-down wagon. *Going to District Four to seek their fortune, most likely.*

Hundreds of peasants had been pouring into District Four, where Demetri's outpost was, spurred by the king's false report that there were jobs and food to be had in the northwest territory of Amarias. *Perhaps I should warn them that they will find nothing more than crowded cities and dry wells.* District Four was just as beaten-down as the rest of the kingdom seemed to be these days.

Demetri took off his boot and hit it against the rock, watching the sand fall to the ground. When the three were dead, he would go back to District Four. He frowned. *And what waits for me there? A lifetime of hiding in the desert. Alone.*

A sound from the wagon nearby made his head jerk up. It was the cry of a little girl, the one from the traveling family. She was helping her father pull a canvas over the wagon for the night, and had tripped over a rock.

Her father rushed to her side and helped her up, examining the small scrape with an appropriate amount of concern and seriousness, then tickling her until her tears turned to laughter. The mother came out from the other side of the wagon, smiling, but telling them to keep quiet and not disturb the other travelers.

Demetri found himself drawn by the scene, and he knew why. It was not because he missed his own parents; his mother had died when he was young, and his father had never made much time for his two sons. But he had dreamed of being a father once, before the disaster.

No. Do not think of her. Think only of the mission. He would find the three Youth Guard members, and they would die. If he failed, Aleric, captain of the Youth Guard, would kill his brother. He could not fail. Completing the mission was what was important now.

That was the problem with journeying alone. There was no one to distract him from his memories, no one to focus his mind on the task at hand.

"Hey there!" Demetri looked up to see an old man poke his head out of a tent nearby. "Don't know if you realize, but curfew's comin'. You ought to put down for the night. Rules are rules here in Amarias."

The captain just nodded at the man. "Thank you for the warning," he called. *It must be too dark for him to notice my*

Patrol uniform. Or else he is too blind.

The old man was right: curfew was coming. The sun had begun to set, and most of the travelers along the road were already hidden away in tents near the mountain trail. *Apparently they do not wish to go far, for fear of the saards.*

Demetri lay down, using his pack for a pillow. *The chase will end tomorrow.*

It didn't take him as long as usual to fall asleep, but the dream was as vivid as ever. He was in his father's courtyard at dawn, before the aurora blossoms on the trellis had opened. The garden felt unfamiliar, like it was from a different life. *Or one I can hardly remember.*

It was strange; Demetri had spent hours studying in the courtyard when he was younger. He recognized every stone in the pavement, every patch of flowers, and even the cracks in the gate. Something was different, though. No birds were singing. The shadows of the trees stretched out into menacing forms. The light from the rising sun seemed dimmer and the scent of the flowers hinted at poison.

By now, Demetri was used to the nightmares, but this one gave him the feeling of being watched. He had felt the same the night in Nalatid, when he had failed the first time to kill the Youth Guard members.

So it did not surprise him when Aleric entered the gate. "They are here," he said simply and without explanation.

"No," Demetri said, daring to contradict his superior. "They can't be. It's impossible."

"You wasted a day of travel by returning to Nalatid," Aleric reminded him. "The time you made up by traveling late into the night was lost the next morning with your exhaustion. You practically stumbled through the desert."

"I couldn't sleep," Demetri said, trying to justify himself. He felt the medallion again. "The dreams...."

Aleric shrugged. "The medallion doesn't cause your nightmares, Captain, although it does allow me to communicate with you. If the medallion produces dark dreams, it is only pulling from the darkness in your own heart."

Then he shook his head. "But there is the matter of this squad. I want them destroyed, Demetri. They worry me, more than many generations of Youth Guard. The prophecy...."

His voice trailed off. "What prophecy?" Demetri pressed.

"It would do little good to tell you," Aleric said, "as you are not a man of superstition."

That was true enough. Demetri let it pass. Strangely, even though the sun was rising, the garden seemed to be getting darker and dimmer. All he could see clearly now was Aleric's face; the rest was in the shadows.

"Captain, you must find them and kill them," Aleric said, his eyes burning into Demetri's mind. "You have no idea what the stakes are. These three, and the one they left behind, could destroy the entire kingdom and more than that."

Demetri frowned. "But they're only young people."

"Only young people!" Aleric hissed. "You underestimate them even now, after all you saw them do in the desert?"

Demetri winced. "Luck. That was all."

"No. I do not think it was." Aleric leaned forward. "Captain, let me explain the seriousness of this situation. I cannot always see them."

That didn't seem very serious to Demetri. "Neither can I. If we could, they would be dead by now."

"Listen, Captain," Aleric said harshly. "I have been given the power to see a vision of anyone I name."

Demetri stared at the old man. The ability was strange and unnatural. Perhaps even evil. *But imagine the power it would give.*

"But with these three…I can only catch glimpses," Aleric went on. "That is why I did not know where they were until now. And I have not yet seen the fourth, the one they left behind. Perhaps he is already dead."

Aleric leaned forward. "There are forces at work here you do not understand, Captain. And I do not expect you to. But what you need to know is that they are being protected. Because of this, more than anything else, they must die."

Suddenly, Demetri was no longer in the garden courtyard. He was standing in a dark, shadowy forest, where three figures, two of them no higher than Demetri's shoulder, were hurrying through the trees. It was them, the three he was sent to find and kill. Demetri knew it without a doubt.

Demetri glanced around. There was the river. Farther, through the trees, the bridge. He knew where he was, and, if the dream was correct, where *they* were. He followed them. In the dream, his every movement was silent. Not a twig snapped, not a leaf rustled.

"Here," the crippled boy, the one with the staff said, pointing. Before them was a run-down shack that looked out-of-place in the middle of the woods.

The tall one with the pale hair stopped. "Did you hear something?"

Even though he was sure it was a dream, Demetri froze. The medallion was burning again, so fiercely that Demetri almost wondered if the three would be able to hear it sizzle as it seared his flesh.

"No," the crippled boy said. "But I wonder...."

He turned around just then and looked straight at Demetri. The boy had green eyes, almost like the ones Demetri had seen many times in his own reflection. For a second, Demetri was sure their eyes met—that the boy could see him.

Demetri awoke, clutching the medallion and staring straight up at the sky. The moon was shining brightly. Demetri wondered how long he had been asleep—how much time he had given the Youth Guard members to escape.

He packed up his supplies silently, so as not to wake the other travelers. He needed more men and the nearest Patrol outpost was three miles from the pass. That would waste time, but he would not underestimate the Youth Guard. Not this time.

CHAPTER 2

Everything about the forest outside of Mir reminded Jesse of home. The familiar sounds, the wind rustling the branches, the distant river, and the sight of the same trees he had seen nearly every day of his life made him feel safe. Even the smell, like moss and wet clay, was comforting.

He took a deep breath. "Doesn't it make you feel like life is almost back to normal?"

Rae, walking silently in front of him, didn't turn around. "Almost," she muttered. "Except for the fact that we're traveling in the dark after curfew, we're exhausted from a trek through the desert, and we're creeping through the trees, trying not to be seen by Patrol members who would kill us on sight."

She paused to sweep aside a low-hanging branch. Jesse ducked to avoid being hit in the face as it snapped back. "Other than those small details, you're exactly right, Jesse."

Well. Someone could use a little sleep. Jesse began to wonder if his great idea had been so great after all.

He had spent a half hour of arguing to convince Silas to continue on after dark. Ever the practical one, Silas had insisted that they spend the night in the forest and continue on to Kayne's cabin at dawn. He had even set up the tents. "I will not allow you to endanger our lives," he had said several times.

After the fifth time, Jesse had unleashed his last argument. "Our lives? What about Parvel's? He is in danger, and he doesn't even know it!"

It was true. Back in the desert, they had learned the Youth Guard, the elite fighting force for the king, really had been created to kill the strongest, most talented young people in the kingdom of Amarias. They were the biggest threat to King Selen's throne, and that was why Jesse, Silas, and Rae were now fleeing for their lives from Captain Demetri and his Patrol.

"It's our fault that Captain Demetri knows where Parvel is staying," Jesse had continued. "We have to get to him before the captain does. How can you stop a mile outside of town?"

Silas had still grumbled his share of doubts and warnings, but in the end had helped Rae and Jesse take down their camp. Now Silas was leading the way, using his sharp vision to guide them through the dark, while making as little noise as possible.

For a moment, Jesse didn't worry about the possibility of being discovered. Instead, he thought about home: seeing Kayne and Parvel again, eating a real meal, and sleeping in a bed instead of on rocks.

The change would be welcome. He, Rae, and Silas had traveled through miles of desert, battling heat, eating stale food, and sleeping on the hard ground. Before that they had been lost, buried, imprisoned, and nearly executed. Jesse was sore and tired and, though he would never admit it to Silas or Rae, homesick.

The trees blocked out almost all of the moonlight, deepening the darkness of the night. They were able to cross the Dell River bridge easily without being seen. No Patrol were stationed there, and all the three had to worry about was staying away from the group of travelers camped by the road. For once, the darkness was their ally.

Of course, Jesse had another reason for wanting to approach Kayne's shack at night. He didn't want anyone in Mir to see him and tell Uncle Tristan his runaway nephew had returned to the village. They might beat him for leaving, then drag him back to the inn to wash the supper dishes. Jesse would not go back to that life again.

Now, in the quiet of the night, everything felt right somehow. Jesse hadn't felt that way since before his parents had disappeared. Even though he knew they were headed for Kayne's rundown cabin, not his parents' farm, Jesse felt like he was going home.

Not even Rae's blunt pessimism could sour Jesse's mood. He said cheerfully, "We'll get there soon enough."

They passed the part of the river where the largest fish liked to swim. Next was the huge kambria tree, good for climbing, and the hollow where Jesse and Eli had spent many summer afternoons sword fighting with sticks.

Eli. The memory of his friend made Jesse wince. His childhood friend, now sixteen, a year older than Jesse, was on another squad in the Youth Guard. Where he was or what mission he was trying to accomplish, Jesse didn't know. But he knew one thing: Captain Demetri had made it clear the king was not just trying to kill Jesse's squad. His goal was to eliminate every Youth Guard member.

Worrying won't do any good, Jesse reminded himself, pushing the thought away. Parvel would tell him to pray, but, except for a few desperate moments during their mission, Jesse refused to have anything to do with that. *Eli can take care of himself.*

Soon they reached the worn leaves and stamped-down dirt that was the only path to Kayne's house. He didn't have many visitors, and he liked it that way.

Years ago, Kayne had moved away from the town. Whenever Jesse asked him why, he would get a strange look on his face and say, "Had to. These days, trees are better neighbors than people. Mark my words, boy, there's evil growing here in Amarias. Can't get away from it outright, but I do what I can."

Jesse had never known quite what to think of that. Now, after all he had learned about the king, it made more sense. *I wonder if Kayne suspected all along.*

Before darting out into the small clearing, Silas paused at the edge of the trees, peering into the darkness. Jesse was glad Silas was being cautious. Rae, with her dark hair and effortless movements, blended in perfectly with the night, but Silas' pale blond hair shone in the moonlight, and Jesse's limp made it hard for him to move quietly. *Not that anyone is watching. They wouldn't be…would they? No one wants to be caught outside after curfew.*

"Here," Jesse said, pointing to Kayne's home like Silas might not have noticed it. The old shack, sagging and groaning in the breeze, looked less than welcoming, but Jesse knew better. He wanted to get inside. The woods felt darker and more dangerous all of a sudden.

Silas started to enter the clearing, then stopped. "Did you hear something?" he asked, staring straight ahead.

Jesse froze and let the soft background noises of the forest fill his ears, the noises he had heard all his life. Silas was right. Something was different. It wasn't a sound, though.

"No," Jesse said slowly. "But I wonder…." He turned around. There was no one there. Nothing moved in the trees except a wing-tipped owl, landing silently on a nearby branch and staring at them. *No one is watching us—at least, no one human.*

Still, Jesse was relieved when Silas nodded and led them out of the trees. The forest wasn't safe; Jesse was sure of that. He remembered the mysterious man who had shot Parvel. Silas thought he was a member of the Rebellion, a group sworn to fight against the king. He was dead, killed by Silas' arrow, but Jesse knew the Rebellion had many members.

What if another one returned to find the rest of us? Jesse shook his head at his thoughts. *It can't be. The Rebellion didn't know we would return at all, much less when.*

They had reached the shadowy building, and Jesse knocked cautiously on the door.

No answer. Jesse's heart began to beat faster, and he pictured the inside of the cabin, ransacked by Rebellion members who had dragged Kayne and Parvel away. Maybe the Patrol found out Kayne had helped Jesse run away and had taken him to prison. Or maybe….

No, Jesse corrected himself. *Kayne is old, and we must have wakened him from sleep. He'll come.*

Sure enough, after what felt like an unbearable wait, Jesse heard the sound of shuffling feet, faint through the thin wood of the door. "Who's there?" the familiar raspy voice barked. "I don't have much kindness for those who interrupt the few hours of sleep an old man can get."

Jesse grinned to himself. *Yes. It's Kayne.*

Instead of answering, Jesse opened the door. Kayne stood in the doorway, holding a candle in one hand and a knife in the other, raised high and ready to strike.

"Kayne," Jesse blurted, before the old man could use the weapon. "It's me, Jesse."

Kayne lowered the knife briefly, then stepped closer, prodding the candle at Jesse's face. "Why, so it is!" he exclaimed, a hint of a smile creasing his wrinkled face. "Ought to have known, it being after curfew and all. Seems you get night confused with day fairly often, boy."

"Where did you get the knife?" Rae asked, glancing at it with a frown of disapproval, most likely for the crude craftsmanship of the blade. The law of Amarias had forbidden peasants to own weapons. Kayne was no friend of the king, yet Jesse was surprised that he had a hidden knife.

"Made it myself," Kayne said grimly, all trace of laughter gone from his face. "Didn't mean to frighten you, but...."

"Never mind that," Jesse interrupted. "Where's Parvel?"

Kayne looked away. Then he looked up, and there was something dark and painful in his eyes. "Jesse, Parvel is gone."

Silas and Rae immediately started firing questions at Kayne, like a barrage of arrows. "Quiet, you fools!" Kayne interrupted sharply. "Would you bring the whole village into the woods?" He motioned them inside.

Although he knew he must have moved, Jesse didn't remember entering Kayne's cabin, placing the packs of supplies down or sitting at the table. All he could do was stare in confusion.

The room still looked the same, welcoming and warm with its tapered candles and carefully crafted furniture. Even the smell, dirt and bark mixed with bittersweet tea, brought back good memories. But something felt terribly wrong.

Rae was the first one to break the silence. "Tell us what happened to him," she commanded. "If he's not here, then where is he?"

Kayne eased into one of the chairs, his ordinary blustering manner gone. "I kept Parvel in my own room all day, out of sight of anyone who might pass by. Not that anyone did, mind you. It was as quiet as ever out here, even quieter with you gone, Jesse."

As far as Jesse knew, he was the only one who ever came to the rundown cabin, taking a few minutes in between chores at the inn to visit the old man. For a moment, Jesse wondered what it would be like to lead a life as lonely as Kayne's. *Having Parvel around must have done him good.*

"I checked on him every hour, changed the poultice, brought him food. A good patient he was. Never complained, even on bad days. He seemed to get better all the time. Even stopped that muttering of his." Kayne shuddered. "That was the worst of it, especially in the middle of the night." He looked up at them. "Then he disappeared."

"When?" Silas demanded. "When was this?"

Kayne seemed to think carefully about this. "Five days ago. Since Parvel was doing well, I let him sleep through the night without checking on him. That morning, when I went in…."

His voice died off. Rae cleared her throat. "What did you find when you went into the room?"

Jesse glared at her. "Can't you see that he's upset?"

"I can speak for myself, thank you," Kayne shot back. He turned to Rae. "Outside of the room, nothing was out of place. But when I opened the door, Parvel wasn't in his bed."

Gone. Just like that, their squad captain had disappeared. *But how? And why?*

"At first I thought he might be getting a drink at the well, or something like that."

"Parvel wouldn't be so foolish," Silas said.

"I didn't think so," Kayne said. "I'd warned him enough. But just a few days before, he'd been a raving lunatic. Never know what those raving lunatics are going to do. I searched everywhere I could think. Didn't find a thing."

"That's all?" Silas asked in disbelief when Kayne stopped talking. Jesse noticed he hadn't touched his food either.

"No," Kayne said, shaking his head. "I went back to the room again—I don't know—maybe thinking he was hiding under the bed. I noticed the sheets were all on the floor, like there had been some kind of struggle. And there was blood."

Jesse couldn't stop himself from gasping.

"How much?" Silas asked, keeping his eyes fixed on Kayne.

"Not a lot." Coming from Kayne, who was the village doctor and had seen buckets of blood in his day, that wasn't very comforting. "I don't think Parvel was killed, and that's not just me being hopeful."

From the look on his face, Jesse knew that Silas desperately wanted to believe him. "Why?"

"Because," Kayne continued, "whoever took Parvel left this behind." He handed Silas a small object.

Jesse and Rae leaned across the table to look at it. It was a gray rock, with flecks of white speckled through it. In the very center was a carving of the king's medallion, marked through with a vicious, deep X. In the half-darkness of the room, it glowed with a strange white light.

"The symbol of the Rebellion," Kayne said, though they all knew it. It was intended to make a mockery of the symbol of Amarias, the same symbol that was branded on the shoulder of every member of the Youth Guard.

"Excellent," Rae said, her voice dripping with sarcasm. "Now the king *and* the Rebellion are trying to kill us."

Kayne stared at her, squinting out of his tiny, dim eyes. "The king?"

"We'll explain later," Silas said, tracing the grooves of the rock in his hand, almost unconsciously. "But you should all know that this stone is more than just the symbol of the Rebellion. It is the symbol of the Rebellion in District Two."

"How so?" Kayne asked.

"Each district has its own distinct customs and way of life," Silas said flatly. Rae, Jesse, and Kayne nodded. They all knew that. "Members of the Rebellion—though they share the common purpose of destroying the king—are slightly different in every district. So are their symbols."

Jesse frowned. "But I know here, in District One, their symbol is the same." Though people rarely spoke of the Rebellion, everyone seemed to know certain things about it from whispered stories or rumors.

"Not a different symbol," Silas corrected himself. "Different materials." He held the stone up. "Rebellion leaders in District Two use the stone of the Deep Mines, common in our range of the Suspicion Mountains. District Four uses the orange sandstone we saw in the Abaktan Desert. District One, known for its farmers and blacksmiths, uses common iron."

"District Three, home to the greatest forests in Amarias, uses wood," Rae finished, speaking of her own home district.

Silas nodded grimly. "So you have seen it, then?"

"Once," Rae admitted. "When the king's storeroom was plundered and all of the deer taken, I saw the symbol carved on the door."

"You know an awful lot about the Rebellion, boy," Kayne said mildly, looking Silas in the eye.

Silas' fist closed around the Rebellion stone, and Jesse could see his jaw tighten. "Is that an accusation?"

"Not a bit," Kayne said. "But you young people seem to have a habit of being more than you appear to be. Care to explain?"

The anger on Silas' face made Jesse shrink back in his chair. But they soon discovered Silas was not angry with Kayne. "I have seen this symbol before," he said, clenching the rock in his fist. "At the place where they murdered my father."

His father? Suddenly, all the hateful things Silas had said about the Rebellion made sense.

"So," Silas said, setting the rock down on the table with a thud, "we know that if Parvel is still alive, he is in the hands of the Rebellion—the Rebellion in District Two, which is far worse."

"Why worse?" Jesse asked.

"Each district has unique tactics," Silas replied. "I've studied them. Those in District Three, for example," he said, nodding at Rae, "often steal from the king and his officials. They rarely resort to violence. Not so in District Two. They are ambitious, well-organized, and harsh. They will do whatever is necessary to accomplish their goals."

"Including traveling to another district to kidnap a lone Youth Guard member?" Jesse asked, not entirely convinced.

"Or kill him," Silas said. Seeing the look on Jesse's face, he hastily added, "But if they had done that, they wouldn't have left a stone; they would have left his body. That would make a far greater impact."

That reasoning didn't make Jesse feel any better. *Even if Parvel is still alive, how can we find him again?*

"I have heard the Rebellion has a stronghold in the ruins of the Deep Mines," Silas said, as if hearing Jesse's unspoken question. "It's very treacherous territory, and few who enter ever return. That is where they would take Parvel."

There was another pause. "Well," Kayne said, standing from the table. "I'd best get you some food, then. It'll be another long trek, and you'll need your strength."

"I take it you think we should go after him, then," Rae said dryly.

Kayne looked at her like she had a stone for a brain. "Of course. While he was here, Parvel was like a member of the family. Reminded me of my own son." Jesse might have imagined it, but he thought he saw the hint of a tear in Kayne's eye.

Kayne set his face in determination. "Even if you're not sure where he is, even if you're not sure he's alive, you have to try to find him."

Jesse glanced at Rae, and she nodded. He knew what Silas' answer would be. Sure enough, Silas nodded solemnly. "We will go." He stood up from the table and added, "Tonight." He kept the Rebellion stone in his hand, gripping it tightly.

Kayne was already rummaging through drawers and in cabinets, finding food to give them for their journey. Jesse just hoped he wouldn't slip in any of the nasty medicinal tea he sometimes brewed.

"I'll draw water for our journey," Silas said. "We'll travel by the river as much as possible, but anything can happen."

Jesse did not like the sound of that. *But, really, we're traveling to the hideout of a faction of radical, ruthless kidnappers. Running out of water would be one of the easier problems to deal with.*

Jesse glanced over at Kayne. He was digging in the medicine cabinet, muttering to himself and pulling out a small canister of tea. Instead of taking out a few leaves, he put the whole thing in the already bulging sack he held. *He must be emptying his entire pantry for us.*

"This will be a short visit," Jesse said, trying to laugh a little, "even for me."

Kayne stopped and glanced up at Jesse. "Some things can't be helped," he said crisply. "You have to go after him. If I thought you'd need an old man to slow you down, I'd go along myself."

Jesse almost laughed, picturing Kayne stumbling along a mountain path on a dangerous mission into Rebellion territory. *Then again*, he mused, *I have very little room to laugh. I'm not much more than a cripple, and I've come this far.*

Kayne set down the sack and gestured toward Jesse's walking stick. Jesse handed it to him, and Kayne held it close to his eyes, examining it. "Hmm. It's been through a lot, hasn't it, Jesse?"

Jesse nodded. "I have many stories. Maybe I can tell you if we come back."

"When," Kayne said, handing the walking stick back to him. "You can tell me *when* you come back, with Parvel. Now, if you want speed, you ought to...."

A loud pounding at the cabin door cut off his words. "Open up, in the name of the king!" a voice shouted. "Patrol here."

Captain Demetri. Jesse's eyes darted to Kayne. "A Patrol captain is searching for us," Jesse explained as quickly as he could.

That seemed to settle the matter for Kayne. "Run," he commanded in a low tone, shoving the sack of supplies at him. "Out the back door! I'll hold them off as long as I can."

Rae had already stood and grabbed their other bags. Her eyes were wide, but she didn't make a sound as she followed Jesse to the small door on the other side of the cabin.

"You in there!" the muffled voice outside the door bellowed. "Open up!"

Before he turned away toward the loud voice, Kayne put a hand on Jesse's shoulder. "God be with you," he whispered.

Jesse blinked in surprise. Kayne had never believed in God, at least, not that he knew of. "Now go!" he said, pushing him toward the door.

There was no time to think, no time to wonder. The pounding continued. Jesse took one look back. Kayne was clearing away the extra dishes, all the while moaning sleepily, "Coming! Can't an old man get his sleep? Or has the king made that illegal too?"

Before Jesse could say his last good-bye, a strong hand pulled him out the door. Jesse almost cried out, until he turned to see Silas beside him. "Into the forest," he whispered. "It looks like we won't get any rest tonight."

CHAPTER 3

At least in the mountains we can't leave a trail, Jesse thought wearily as he stumbled along the Way of Tears, the rocky road that led to District Two. *That's better than when we were running from Captain Demetri in…the place with sand in it.* He tripped over a rock in the path. *The desert. That's what it's called.*

Even though his body kept going, step by step, Jesse knew his mind couldn't last much longer. They had been running, then walking, all night, with only one brief rest. Jesse had fallen asleep even in those few minutes before Silas had pulled him to his feet.

"Once they search the place and realize we're not there, they'll come after us," Silas warned. "And if they catch us, they'll kill us."

His blunt words had broken through the haze of exhaustion that hung over Jesse like fog in the early morning. Fear was what made Jesse keep going, leaning heavily on his walking stick. Despite Silas' words, he had not seen or heard anyone following them. *Not that my mind is very sharp right now.*

How do they do it? he wondered, staring at Rae and Silas, who were a short distance ahead of him. If they had slowed since leaving Mir, he hadn't noticed.

The sky was getting lighter, and Jesse heard the birds begin to come out, like they did every morning.

Morning. They had walked all night.

"Silas, wait," he called, his words sounding stiff and lifeless even to his own ears. Silas turned around. "We need to rest. It's almost…." *What is it called when the sun comes up?* "Dawn," he finished. "It's almost dawn."

"He's right," Rae agreed, and Jesse blinked in surprise. *I'm right?* "We should not be out in the open during the day. We can continue on tomorrow night."

"But where can we go?" Jesse asked, working up the energy to move his head around. Nothing but the towering Suspicion Mountains on either side.

"Just a little farther," Silas said, continuing on. "The sign said we passed into District Two."

The sign. There was a sign, wasn't there?

"The Deep Mines are just ahead," Silas informed them. "I know of a place there where no one will find us."

He and Rae said other things, but Jesse stopped listening. All he knew was that he was not allowed to sleep yet. He groaned and followed the other two, feeling angry with them, but not remembering why. He kept Silas' words in his mind. *Just a little farther.*

Most of the "little farther" was blurred in Jesse's memory. Once, he must have fallen asleep, because his bleary eyes woke to Rae pouring cold water over his face. She helped him to his feet and dragged him along. He let her, because it would have been too much work to pull away.

From then on, he just focused on the bottom of his walking stick, placing it down on the ground, then picking it up again. He found a steady rhythm after a while, until Silas tore his attention away from the all-important task.

"Here," Silas said, pointing at a grove of trees at one end of a canyon. "Welcome to Urad."

What's Urad? Does Urad mean sleep?

Jesse followed Silas toward the trees, then through them. Finally, they stopped in front of a patch of thick brambles and thorns. Silas stooped to crawl, but Jesse decided not to follow.

I can sleep here just as well as…wherever Silas is going.

From behind him, Rae muttered some kind of threat, which Jesse's tired mind didn't understand. Then she shoved him into the brambles, which Jesse did understand. The shock of pain roused him enough to make him crawl after Silas.

The ground was hard, and his lame leg throbbed with the pressure. The briars seemed to go on forever. Then, Silas stopped and pulled aside a thick curtain of moss to reveal a dark hole in the side of the mountain.

But that's not possible…is it? Maybe I'm already dreaming.

"We're here," Silas said, crawling into the cave.

Jesse would have smiled—he would have jumped up and down with joy—but that would have taken far too much energy. Somewhere in the back of his mind, Jesse remembered he didn't like small, dark caves that looked threatening, but he was too tired to care.

The cave was dark and cool inside. The rocks were hard, but that didn't bother Jesse. He laid his pack down for a pillow and collapsed on the ground by the entrance. Rae and Silas were talking again. *They can tell me in the morning* was his last thought before he fell asleep.

When he next opened his eyes, the cave was glowing with golden light. He sat up and brushed away the moss from the cave entrance, looking outside. A few brave flecks of sunlight made their way through the thicket of thorns surrounding the cave. *Early afternoon,* Jesse guessed.

"A nice place to rest, isn't it?" Silas asked. Jesse turned around to face him. He was leaning against the wall, a bit deeper into the cave where the light was dimmer and the shadows longer.

"Any place would have been a good place to rest," Jesse said, rubbing the sleep out of his eyes.

A slight smile twitched at the corner of Silas' mouth. "Yes, I was afraid we were going to have to carry you the rest of the way."

We. "Where's Rae?"

"She insisted on going on a scouting foray," Silas said. "I think she just wanted to get out of the cave. Like I told her, it's hardly necessary. Even if Captain Demetri did manage to follow us, he is from District Four. This cave is secure, and, more importantly, obscure. Urad is little known outside of District Two."

"This place has a name?"

Silas nodded. "There used to be a city here in these caverns that marked the start of the Deep Mines. But these far eastern mines were abandoned long ago."

"A city underground?" That seemed strange to Jesse.

"Not underground," Silas said. "Just inside the mountain. The Roarics felt safer here, surrounded by rock."

The Roarics. Jesse had heard of them before, but he couldn't remember where.

Jesse tried to stand and nearly hit his head on the ceiling of the cave. He settled for stooping, walking a little farther into the cave. Although the light was dim, the only things Jesse could see beside dirt and rocks were two large wooden pillars supporting the roof of the cavern. "I don't see any evidence of a city."

"It was deeper in. We would need to go through many tunnels and caverns to reach it, I'd wager. But even then, you wouldn't find much to look at. Urad was destroyed."

"Who destroyed it?"

"Patrol members." Silas yawned loudly. He was clearly already bored with the subject. "Or, actually, more like a small army of Patrol, I'd guess."

That wasn't answer enough for Jesse. "But why? What happened?"

Silas shrugged. "Some kind of treason, I suppose. It happened years before I was born. Why does it matter?"

"I don't know. It's part of a story."

"So?"

Jesse tried to think of a way to explain himself without sounding foolish. *How do you tell someone who only thinks in terms of facts and strategies why it's important to hear stories?* Eventually, he gave up. "I just wanted to know."

There was silence in the cave for a minute. "Who were the Roarics?" Jesse asked, almost timidly.

"A race of dwarves. Hardy and strong. They worked in this section of the mine years ago, before they were wiped out." As always, Silas answered patiently, even though it was clear he didn't care.

An entire race wiped out, a city destroyed, and he doesn't even know why? Jesse could hardly understand. It was frustrating, the lack of value those in District Two put on stories.

Jesse sat down by the entrance. Although the cave seemed safe enough, he preferred the sunlight to the dark shadows. This was not what he had planned on back in the woods outside of Mir. *Well, we made it home, for a few moments at least.*

To be honest, Jesse was tired of traveling, tired of running from the king's men, tired of saying good-bye to the people he loved, not sure if they would ever meet again.

Jesse thought of Kayne's strange parting words, "God be with you." Not strange, for some in Amarias, perhaps, although few cared much about religion these days. But Jesse and his family had always been self-sufficient, and Kayne even more so.

Kayne had always looked after Jesse, especially after his parents disappeared. He had been the only one in Mir who hadn't believed they abandoned him. Though gruff and hardened by life, Kayne was a good man. "That's my religion," he said. "Doing the right thing without a god to make me do it."

So why would Kayne refer to a God he didn't believe in? *It had to be because of Parvel.* Parvel was a firm believer in God, one of those who called themselves Christians, and had stayed with Kayne for nearly two weeks. Naturally, Kayne would pick up some of his phrases.

But he can't actually believe in that nonsense, can he? Jesse just couldn't understand the idea of worshiping an invisible God. *Maybe some divine figure created the world, but a personal, invisible God who protects humans? That's too much for me.*

Jesse heard the sound of someone crashing through the brambles outside the cave, interrupting his thoughts.

"It's probably Rae," Silas whispered, backing deeper into the cave. "But, just in case…."

Jesse followed, and they both crouched behind a boulder in the darker part of the cave. "Silas!" Rae's voice called. The tone of her voice gave Jesse a sick feeling. *There must be trouble.*

They peered out from behind the rock to see Rae tumble into the cave, out of breath. "Silas, Jesse, where are you?"

"Here," Silas called, stepping from behind the rock. He hit his head on the roof of the cavern, and Jesse had to stop himself from laughing.

Rae's words took all thoughts of laughter away. "They're here," Rae said, panting. "They're here, and they know about the cave. I was above them, on the cliffs, and I heard them talking…." She paused to catch her breath. "Somehow, they found our trail. I don't understand it. But they will find us here."

Silas nodded, and Jesse could practically see his mind moving behind his gray eyes. "How far away are they?"

"Only a few minutes behind. I ran here as fast as I could."

"We can't keep running from them," Silas said grimly.

"They must have a tracking expert with them. And if they know about the cave…."

"You said there are tunnels here," Jesse interrupted. "In the dark, they would have a hard time following us."

"That's true," Silas said, nodding.

Jesse almost wished Silas hadn't agreed. He had never liked the dark. *Especially if there's anything else living in these tunnels.* He had heard stories of cave creatures with white, blind eyes that would attack based on scent alone.

Silas dropped to his knees and ripped open his supply pack. "We'll have to proceed slowly so we don't fall into any pits." He held up the flint triumphantly. "This will help."

"And what do you suggest we light?" Jesse pointed out. He noticed Silas' eyes on his staff, and he jerked it back, clutching it protectively. "I'd let you set my head on fire first!"

"Let's have it, then."

Jesse wasn't entirely sure Silas was joking. Thankfully, Rae provided an alternative. She hurried into the darkness, feeling along the cave wall. "Here!"

Rejoining them, she presented Silas with a stick of wood fitted into an iron holder. "Your torch, sir," she said, giving him a mock bow.

"How did you find this?" Jesse asked. He fingered the metal holder. Its surface was tarnished from years of disuse, but he could still see the rough design of a boar's head formed by the iron.

"I woke up early and explored the cave while you and Silas were still sleeping," Rae said, shrugging.

Of course she did. Jesse was sure Rae never ran out of energy. He was surprised she slept at all.

Silas lit the torch, and the resulting glow made Jesse feel slightly safer. "Come on," Silas said, holding the torch in front of him as he made his way into the shadows of the cave.

Rae bit her lip, for once not following immediately behind him. "And you're sure the ghosts of the Roarics are just a local superstition?"

"What?" Jesse blurted.

Rae glanced at Jesse. "Silas didn't tell you?"

"No," Jesse said, glaring at Silas in the dark. "He failed to mention ghosts."

Silas shrugged. "I've heard that people from District One are superstitious, and I didn't want to worry you."

"Oh, because I'm far less worried now that we're running from a Patrol of armed guards into a dark pit haunted by ghosts," Jesse shot back.

"See. I knew you'd be upset."

"Well, *I'll* be upset if Captain Demetri and his men shoot arrows through us while we stand here talking," Rae snapped. Clearly, she'd rather risk ghosts than stay still, doing nothing. "Come on."

Although Silas led the way with the torch, Rae and Jesse had an easier time scrambling through the passageways, since both were nearly a head shorter than their leader. *I never thought I would be grateful to be short,* Jesse thought, as Silas bumped his head on a low outcropping for the third time.

Jesse had a hard time getting a good look at the cave, since he was forced to walk with a slight stoop, but there were signs that the tunnels had clearly once been home to a civilized people group. Here and there a torch was lashed to the wall, and the stone nearby was darkened from soot. Jesse spotted a threshing floor for wheat, and a broken piece of pottery. Once, he saw something like a well, but Silas wouldn't let him stop to examine it.

"We may need water if we run out of supplies," Jesse pointed out.

"We have plenty in the packs," Silas reminded him. "Now keep walking and stop talking."

Jesse did stop talking, but for a different reason. *The packs.* He felt his back, just to make sure. The pack of supplies was not there. Jesse could see the pack in his mind, almost as if he were actually looking at it. It was laying beside the mouth of the cave. *That will be the first thing Captain Demetri sees when he and his men reach the cave.*

Ahead of him, Silas had stopped. *I have to tell him. But how?* Jesse could hardly picture Silas' reaction, but he was sure he would be furious. *And Rae, she'll be even more angry. Oh, why? Why did it have to be me?*

Feeling like some ancient curse had turned his feet into the same stone that formed the cave walls, Jesse joined Silas and Rae. "Silas…."

"Shh," he hissed, not looking back at him. Jesse glanced up to see that he and Rae were staring at something in the tunnel in front of them.

A light was glowing dimly from behind a large rock formation that nearly blocked the path.

"Maybe one of the Roarics forgot to blow out his torch," Jesse said, half-jokingly. But the light flickered strangely, almost like it really was another torch. *Ghosts don't exist... do they?*

"I'll look," Rae volunteered, her hand lightly brushing against the hilt of her sword. "Maybe there's a hole that lets in light from the surface."

"No," Silas warned, drawing his bow. In his hurry, he hit his head on the ceiling for the fourth time. "Wait for us!" But Rae had already stepped forward, darting behind the rock.

In the next second, her scream echoed in the cave.

"Rae!" Silas and Jesse shouted together, taking the few steps to the formation in running leaps.

"Don't move," a strange, deep voice commanded.

Jesse froze. *Captain Demetri?*

But the person who stepped from behind the rocks—a torch in one hand and a spear, which he held to Rae's throat, in the other—looked nothing like the Patrol captain. He was a dwarf, one who barely came to Rae's shoulders, and he had a long, dark beard and fierce eyes. His clothes seemed to be nothing more than a collection of rags, wrapped around him and tied with a length of rope.

If he is a ghost, he doesn't look like I imagined one would. The Roaric did look fierce and very annoyed by their presence, none of which was good for Rae, who seemed to be trying not to breathe.

"Please, take your spear away," Silas said, slowly and calmly. He had also stopped at the Roaric's command. "We mean you no harm."

The Roaric's eyes darted to the bow Silas held at the ready. Silas, understanding his meaning, dropped his weapon.

"Jesse," Silas said, never looking away from Rae and the Roaric, "put down your sword."

"Oh." Since he had never used it, Jesse often forgot he carried a sword at all. He pulled it clumsily from his sheath and let it clatter to the ground.

"You," the Roaric said, nodding at Jesse. "Take her sword."

"You mean Rae's?" Jesse asked. He immediately felt foolish. *What other "hers" are there in this cave?* He practically had to pry Rae's fingers away from the hilt to get at it—her hands were frozen like the expression of fear on her face.

"Who are you?" Jesse asked, still not convinced the Roaric in front of him, *for that must be what he is,* was not a ghost.

"My name is Bern, of the hunter clan," he replied tersely. "And you are my prisoners. You will follow me."

He yanked Rae forward, still holding his spear close to her.

"Where are we going?" Jesse ventured. Silas glared at him, clearly not wanting him to irritate their captor.

Bern looked at him in disbelief, as if it should be obvious. "To New Urad, of course."

CHAPTER 4

Tunnels cut through the dark stone of the cave like a maze. It reminded Jesse, strangely, of the lair of a giant worm, burrowing deep into the ground. *We would have been able to lose Captain Demetri and the Patrol easily down here,* he thought.

As he watched Bern the Roaric march Rae forward at the end of his spear, Jesse decided it was better to be in his hands than in the captain's. *Maybe he'll let us go when he discovers we were only taking shelter in the cave.*

As they stooped through another fork in the tunnel, Jesse asked, "Where do all these tunnels lead?"

Bern did not look back at him. "Many places. Wine-presses. Grain storage. Wells. Blacksmiths. Weavers. Most of them abandoned now."

"But so many tunnels?"

"All of the Deep Mines are like this," Bern said. "That is what I have heard. I have never traveled from this cave."

Although his words were clipped and gruff, he seemed perfectly willing to talk to his captives. *Almost as if he hasn't had anyone to talk to for a while.*

The thought had occurred to Jesse that Bern might be the lone survivor of the massacre Silas had talked about, or perhaps one of a few. *The Patrol couldn't have killed everyone, not with so many places to run.*

Again, he wondered what the Roarics had done to deserve such a harsh punishment. "Some kind of treason," Silas had said. That explanation did not predict good things for them. *If the Roarics rebelled against the king, how will they treat members of the Youth Guard, the king's special fighting force?*

The more they walked, the more convinced Jesse was that Bern wouldn't need to hold Rae hostage. *We would never be able to find our way back anyway.*

After they passed an archway carved with strange symbols, Jesse notice a kind of path, marked with glowing stones. He stooped to look at one of them. Gray stone with white flecks. "Silas," he said, excitedly, "this is the same rock your Rebellion stone was made of!"

Silas just pulled him up. "Come on," he hissed. "He'll think you're trying to run away!"

"I just wanted to…."

"Rae could be hurt because of your foolish dawdling!" Silas shoved him forward, making Jesse scrape his head on the rock.

"What are these stones?" Jesse asked, hoping Bern would know the answer.

This time, Bern stopped and glanced back at Jesse. "You Above-grounders ask many questions."

"Not all of us," Silas said dryly.

"We in New Urad rarely ask questions," Bern said. Jesse

didn't think Bern was being critical; he was simply stating a fact.

"We used to mine these stones for the king before the Fall," he continued. "In New Urad, they are the only light at all."

Jesse frowned. *Imagine living life in a stone prison, with only glowing rocks for light.*

He knew he would hate it. It was hard enough for him to walk in the near-darkness of the cave, and he had only been there for one day. *The problem is not being able to see where I'm going*, Jesse decided. *I don't like stepping out into the dark.*

All of a sudden, Rae gasped, and Jesse jerked his head up. But Bern hadn't brought the spear closer to her. She had merely stepped through another archway, this one twice as large as the first.

Silas and Jesse followed, and Jesse stretched, grateful to be able to stand up straight.

Then he looked around, and almost gasped too. Here, the narrow tunnel exploded into a huge cavern, high enough to allow six Patrol members to stand on each others' shoulders, and large enough to fit....

A small village. "This must be Urad," Jesse said in awe.

"Yes," Bern agreed. "The ruins of it." Perhaps because they had no weapons, or perhaps because they made no move to run back the way they came, Bern lowered his spear and let them gape at their surroundings.

A second glance showed the extent of Urad's destruction. As if they had been thrown about at random, piles of the glowing rocks illuminated the sad remains of charred buildings, broken pottery, and scattered straw.

"No one from Above-ground has seen this place since the Fall," Bern said softly, almost as if he might disturb some sacred relics.

Rae ran over to one of the homes, picking up a half-burnt piece of wood. She studied it for a second. "Black pine," she said. "From the forests of District Three." Her voice sounded almost wistful, and Jesse suddenly realized she missed her home as much as he missed his.

"Come back," Bern said, sounding a bit unsure, as if he was afraid Rae would run off.

"I'll stay behind," Jesse volunteered. *Bern must know more of the story than Silas did.*

Bern nodded at Rae and Silas, and Jesse sat down beside the archway, leaning against the cold stone. Bern remained standing, spear at the ready and eyes fixed straight ahead.

Jesse took the time to get a good look at their captor. His face was normal, except for the eyes, which were buried in wrinkles. He looked like a person used to squinting in the dark. Although the rags he wore were torn and frayed, they were clean, as was Bern himself. Somehow, Jesse had pictured the Roarics as being filthy, rough cave dwellers, but Bern's face was washed, his beard neatly trimmed, and his boots shined. *He probably looks better than we do.*

Jesse decided to break the silence. "This 'Fall' you talk about," he began, "when did it happen?"

"A long time ago," Bern replied, still staring at the city.

He didn't volunteer any more information, so Jesse continued, "What happened here, Bern? Who destroyed Urad?"

There was a pause. "I cannot say," he replied. "When we

get to New Urad, you may ask the History Keeper. That is his burden to bear."

The History Keeper? Jesse shook his head. *That means there is at least one other survivor, probably more.*

"We must continue to the mines," Bern called. Once Silas and Rae rejoined them, he led them to the opposite side of the cavern.

Jesse felt strange walking through the city ruins. He saw shards of shattered glass, burned furniture, pieces of stone and wood and pottery. *It's like walking on broken fragments of lives.*

One thing he didn't see were the remains of victims of the Fall. "Why aren't there any bones?" Jesse asked.

Immediately, Bern stopped in the path. "They were buried," he said, his voice sounding distant and without emotion. "After the chaos had died down, the survivors came up and buried them, laying them in crypts in the deepest parts of the mines."

Jesse shivered and hoped they wouldn't go to those tunnels. He didn't want to be greeted by Roaric skeletons staring out at him from the dark.

Bern turned to face him, slowing down a little and letting his spear drop. For the first time, Jesse saw emotion in his deep, squinting eyes: pain. "There were so many who died...."

Then, Bern gave an abrupt shake of his head, and his eyes again became blank. He began to walk again, this time faster. "But it is not my burden to bear. It happened long ago. It does not matter now."

One thing is sure, Jesse decided as he stepped over a pile of rubble, *I will have many questions to ask this History Keeper.*

Bern stopped as they were almost to the edge of the ruins, tilting his head back where they came. "I hear voices," he said simply.

Though he heard nothing, Jesse's eyes widened. *Captain Demetri. It has to be.*

"There are others," Jesse said hurriedly, his words slurring together. "Other humans. Evil ones. They're following us."

Bern just grunted and held his spear high, toward Rae again. "No, you fool," Rae snapped. "This is no rescue party–they wouldn't care if you threatened me."

"They've come to kill us," Jesse said, "and then they'll kill you too."

That, at least, Bern understood. "To the mines," he said, hurrying as fast as his short legs would take him through a second, smaller archway. This one was made of the same glowing stone that lined the tunnels.

Jesse followed, but Silas pulled the dwarf back. "We cannot run from them," he said firmly. "They will not stop until they find us, even if they have to search these caverns for days."

"And if you try to give us up to them, we'll tell them about you and your people," Silas said. "They are Patrol."

Bern winced at the word. Clearly, he remembered something about the destruction of Urad.

"They will try to wipe you out again," Silas continued. "Do you really think you can defend yourselves from them?"

Jesse began to feel nervous. Now, even he could hear shouts as the Patrol members found tunnels hidden in the shadows and called for others to join them. They were wasting precious seconds.

Silas must have known it too, because he spoke more quickly. "We have to block the tunnel somehow. Keep them from getting to us. It is the only way."

Bern looked confused, glancing from Silas to the tunnel and back again. The voices got louder. "Yes," he finally said. "Come."

Bern led them into what Jesse guessed were the mines, although he didn't see the deep pits he imagined were a part of mines. There were, however, mangled pickaxes and other supplies scattered about, and a few large, overturned carts. Bern began picking through the rubble, muttering to himself.

"Stay here," Bern said tersely. Jesse noticed he was no longer holding his spear. Instead, he clutched a small barrel in one hand and the torch in the other. Without another word, he ran back into the tunnel.

Jesse started to follow, but Silas shook his head. "Let him go. He seems to know what he's doing."

Jesse wasn't so sure, but Silas seemed confident enough, so he didn't move. Rae paced the cave nervously, while Silas bent down and picked up Bern's spear. He tested the point carefully. "Silas…." Jesse warned.

"Do you want to give it back to him?" Silas pointed out. "He was threatening to kill Rae."

"Just don't do anything foolish," Jessie warned. Silas stiffened, but gave a slight nod.

A few seconds later, Bern came running back. "Under the Miner's Supply," he shouted, pointing at a thick steel overhang jutting out of the stone wall. A few wooden boards attached to framework hung like a mouth full of broken teeth. The rest was ash and debris. *It's a building of some sort*, Jesse decided, *or at least, it was.*

Only the roof, welded to the rock wall and held up by a few metal supports, was still intact. Bern threw his torch to the ground and stomped it out, then ran to one of the overturned carts, pulling it under the steel overhang.

"You," Bern said, nodding at Silas, who was closest to him. "Help me!" He saw the spear in Silas' hand and froze, fear flickering in his squinty eyes. For a moment they stood there, looking at each other.

Then Silas threw down the spear and joined Bern at the cart. The strain on Silas' face indicated the carts were heavier than they appeared. Jesse dropped his own torch to run over and push. Rae was soon beside him.

"What did you do, Bern?" Jesse demanded as they shoved the cart under the overhang.

Bern just shook his head. He grunted and lifted one edge of the cart up, straining with effort. "Get under the cart."

From his urgent tone, Jesse decided that now was not the time for questions. Silas fell to the ground on both knees, then scrambled over to the cart. Once underneath, he crouched and bore some of the weight on his shoulders. "Hurry," he said, groaning.

Jesse let Rae go first, then crawled in after her, dragging his walking stick with him. Bern was last, and then Silas dropped the cart over them with one last grunt of effort.

With none of the glowing stones on the ground, it was pitch black under the cart. Rae's boot jutted into Jesse's back, and he could hear everyone breathing in the silence. *How long will the air last under here?*

Then, suddenly, the entire cave seemed to shake with a violent explosion. The ground rumbled underneath them, and a roar echoed in the cavern. Someone—Bern, Jesse guessed—moaned loudly.

They had asked Bern for a cave-in, and he had given them one. Almost without thinking, Jesse shot his arms out, bracing them against the side of the cart. *As if that will help when hundreds of tons of rock come crashing down on us.*

The entire world collapsed. At least that's what it sounded like from underneath the cart. Jesse imagined the noise he heard was what it would sound like if a thunderstorm rained rock. The ground kept trembling, not a steady, even trembling, but one with punctuated jerks from the impact of the falling boulders.

And yet, only a few rocks bounced off of the overturned cart, and those hit from the side. Bern was muttering something to himself, but Rae and Silas remained silent, hardly breathing.

Jesse was slightly less calm. His trembling hands were still braced against the iron cart, and he felt like screaming at the top of his lungs. Since that would use up most of the air they had left, he settled instead for clutching his walking stick in a white-knuckled grip.

The roar gradually died away, becoming nothing more than a sifting of dust and pebbles plinking against the cart. "All right," Bern said, after what seemed to be years. "We can go out now."

Silas pushed the cart off of them, bearing the weight of the cart on his shoulders. "Go," he grunted.

Jesse hesitated for a second, not wanting to be crushed by a stray rock the moment he crawled from the cart. *And do what? Let Rae go first?* Jesse scolded himself for being so timid and scrambled out.

The mines were in even greater disarray than they had been before. Stone cluttered the neatly marked path, and one large boulder had crashed down on a cart, denting it nearly to the ground. *I'm glad we weren't in that one.*

Yet, the metal overhang they had been under still stood strong, though fallen rocks lay all around it. "Good Roaric metalwork," Bern said, sounding satisfied.

Clearly, though, the worst of the cave-in had not occurred in the mines. Jesse saw the worst when he followed Bern to the tunnel. There, past the archway, a wall of stone blocked the way back.

"What did you do?" Jesse asked again, staring at the dwarf in awe.

"We have a powder that can blast through rock," he explained. "That is how the mines were created, long ago."

"Of course," Silas said, nodding. "I have heard of it."

Bern shrugged. "I am not of the miner clan. I did not know how much to use. So we hid under the cart."

He could have killed himself and us, Jesse realized. If Bern was shaken by the cave-in, he didn't show it.

"Come," he said, turning back toward the mines. "The shaft is just beyond Miner's Supply."

"Maybe we don't want to go with you," Rae pointed out. "After all, you held a spear to my throat." She glanced significantly at Bern, and the rest of her meaning was clear. *The spear you no longer have.*

"You must follow me," Bern said simply, nodding at the heap of rubble that was once the way to the ruins of Urad. "You can't go back now."

CHAPTER 5

The shaft Bern had mentioned was just a rough hole in the ground that had been dug by Roaric miners. At least Jesse assumed they had dug it. Bern didn't know what the shaft was originally used for—just that it now held the iron stairs leading to New Urad.

Jesse did not feel comfortable descending into the ground. But, like Silas had muttered to a very agitated Rae, "We have a better chance of survival by following Bern peacefully."

Even though the glowing stones provided enough light to see the stairs, Jesse still tested each step with his walking stick. *This deep in the mines, there might be pits and holes anywhere.*

Then, abruptly, the stairs stopped. Jesse tried to imagine how far down into the ground they were, then shuddered. *Focus on getting to the surface.*

At the bottom of the stairs was a small archway, which Silas, at least, had to stoop to enter. "Welcome to New Urad," Bern said simply, leading them into a small cavern.

A quick scan of the buildings of New Urad told Jesse

the city's population had shrunk drastically. Only two-dozen homes, all of them tiny and shabby, crouched against the rock. Jesse took a closer look at one nearest the path and saw burn marks scarring the wood.

They built their homes out of rubble from the original Urad, he realized.

No people were in the dwellings or sitting outside of them. Jesse got the strange feeling he was walking through another set of ruins, until Bern led them to the center of the city. Standing quietly in a town square of sorts were the Roaric dwarves of New Urad.

The dwarves turned to look at the procession of strangers as they passed, but only the youngest began to whisper. The rest looked away and returned their attention to the platform, where a female Roaric stood, addressing the people.

"Kasha, of the ruling clan," Bern muttered. He had straightened to attention and held his head high as he led them through the crowd to the platform.

"…Rations this month will be slightly smaller than last," Kasha was saying. "Reports from the hunter clan show that…."

Bern cleared his throat, and the woman looked down at him. She expressed only the slightest surprise at seeing three ragtag Above-grounders with him and motioned him to join her on the platform.

"Go on," Bern said gruffly, shuffling them up three short steps onto the platform. He stood back in the shadows, clearly not used to the attention.

Jesse, Silas, and Rae stood in front of Kasha, waiting for her to question them. Dozens of faces looked up at them.

Although Jesse could see they were all different ages and had different features, they all had squinting eyes, just like Bern. *And no wonder.* Without torches, the only light came from the glowing stones that paved the streets of New Urad. *I imagine the first Urad was the same before it was destroyed.*

No questions came. *Maybe it's customary for strangers to introduce themselves first.*

Apparently Silas thought the same, because he stepped forward. "Greetings," Silas said, his voice echoing in the hollow cavern, "I am Silas, of Davior in District Two, and these are my friends Rae and Jesse. We stumbled into this cave by accident on a journey. Bern found us near the entrance. We are merely lost travelers who mean you no harm." He paused, clearly not sure what else to say.

Jesse hoped Bern wouldn't mention the cave-in and the Patrol members who were chasing them. *That would be hard to explain after Silas' story about "lost travelers."*

The Roaric woman, Kasha, stepped toward them. "It is good that Bern brought you here," she said, nodding at them. "We have not seen one from Above-ground since the Fall."

"And when was that?" Jesse asked, not able to help himself. *Maybe she knows the history of her people.*

She sighed, as if adding up the years took too much effort. "Twenty-six years ago."

Jesse blinked. From the way Bern talked, Jesse thought centuries had passed since Urad was first destroyed. Then he cleared his throat. "Would you like to hear news of what has happened Above-ground during that time?"

Kasha stared at him blankly. "It does not concern us."

Jesse scanned the crowd in disbelief, but not one face looked eager to hear from the Above-grounders. Kasha was clearly not alone in her opinion. "But it might. A new king rules now, one who might not remember your offense…whatever it was."

Jesse hoped that might prompt the leader to explain what had caused the destruction of Urad. Her hair, twisted into a coil at the back of her head, was gray. *Surely she was old enough to understand what happened only twenty-six years ago.*

But Kasha did not say anything. Instead, she stared at them, squinting in thought. At last, she sighed. "No one must know of this place, or the Fall will occur again."

"We won't tell anyone," Jesse offered lamely. He looked to Bern for support, but the younger dwarf was looking humbly at the ground in the presence of his leader.

"No," Kasha said calmly. "You will stay here with us in New Urad. We cannot risk letting you return to the surface."

At that, Rae stiffened and looked to Silas. *She couldn't stand to be trapped down here for the rest of her life*, Jesse knew.

"That won't be necessary, Kasha," a voice from the back of the crowd said. As if by magic, the Roarics parted to show a young dwarf, standing beside one of the dwellings. His face was different than the others in two immediately noticeable ways: he was clean shaven, and he wore a slight smile.

"We have nothing to fear from them," the young dwarf said. Although he was talking to Kasha, he was looking straight at Jesse.

Kasha glanced at them, her squinting eyes cloudy. It seemed to Jesse that she was looking through them, or past them, instead. "But…."

"Kasha," the young dwarf said quietly. "My father's judgment never failed you, even through our darkest hours, though you may not remember. Trust me, I beg you."

There was silence in the cavern for a moment. "Yes," Kasha said slowly. She turned to Jesse. "You will go with the History Keeper. It is decided." As one, all of the Roarics in the group, young and old, nodded their confirmation.

Bern followed them as they stepped down from the platform. "Thank you," Jesse said to him, before they walked over to join the History Keeper. "For saving our lives, I mean." Bern just nodded crisply at him before joining the crowd of Roarics, who now stared fixedly at the platform.

"Come," the History Keeper said. "We must go to a place where we can speak freely."

He led them through the straight, orderly streets, past shacks that looked like a heavy sigh would make them collapse.

"I think we'll be all right," Rae whispered to them. "He stood up for us in front of everyone."

Silas shook his head. "No. I don't trust him."

Jesse said nothing, choosing instead to watch the History Keeper, who was now a few paces ahead of them. *I imagine that all Roarics, deprived of much of their sense of sight, have excellent hearing.* But if he heard them, the History Keeper did not say anything.

The History Keeper stopped at the very back of the cavern, in front of a dwelling set into the stone wall. Jesse noticed it was a distance away from all of the others. "Much different than what you're used to, of course," he said, turning to them, "but it's home."

"So you're the History Keeper," Jesse said thoughtfully, looking him over. He seemed much like the other Roarics. Same rags, same pale skin, same squinty eyes…. *But no. The eyes are not the same, somehow.*

"Yes," the History Keeper said, "that is my title. But you may call me Noa." He sighed and looked away briefly. "It would be nice if someone did."

Jesse blurted out what he was thinking. "I expected someone…older."

"An ancient relic hunched over faded manuscripts, no doubt," Noa said, laughing. "No, although the History Keeper before me, my father, came close to that description." He waved them in through the door. "Come in, please."

"Not yet," Silas said, planting his feet firmly and crossing his arms. "First tell us why you stood up for us at the meeting."

Noa turned his squinting eyes to Silas, looking up at him without judgment. That's when Jesse realized what was different about his eyes. *They have something behind them.*

"You are right to be cautious," Noa said at last. "But, believe me, I mean you no harm. I simply do not trust the ruling clan to make a wise decision about you."

Rae grunted. "No wonder. That Kasha woman would have imprisoned us here for the rest of our lives!"

"Because her own life is built on fear," Noa said. "All these years, my father tried to get the other Roarics to see that, but they would not believe him. Sometimes, I wonder if they were even listening." He shook his head. "I am sorry. We do not need to stand here and talk. Come inside."

This time, even Silas followed, although reluctantly. Noa's dwelling was brighter inside than the dim streets of New Urad, and Jesse blinked and waited for his eyes to adjust before looking around. When he did, he was surprised at what he saw.

One wall was made entirely of the glowing stones that provided the cavern's light. A solitary bench stood on one side of the room, and a makeshift desk on the other, crowded with ancient-looking books. A ragged blanket roll lay beside it.

But what caught Jesse's eyes most of all were the paintings—rows of parchments attached to the wooden wall with iron nails. Each seemed to bear a different, intricate design. He stepped toward them to get a better look in the dim light. The lines were dark and smooth, with shades of color here and there. "These are beautiful," he breathed, tracing one of the outlines.

"They are the histories of Urad," Noa said simply.

"Then you can tell us what happened," Jesse said eagerly, turning to him.

Noa just stared at him, and for a moment, Jesse was afraid he was wrong, or that he had misspoken in some way. "You really want to know?" Noa said at last.

"Yes."

The smile lighting Noa's face was grateful and sad at the same time. "None of the Roarics care to hear the histories," he explained. "Really, they don't care to talk to me at all, shunning me as they did my father before me. But at least my father had me. He told me the histories almost every night."

For a moment, Noa's face showed deep sadness. Jesse thought he understood. Even though he didn't know if his parents were alive or not, he knew what it was like to lose a father.

"Now that he is gone," Noa continued, "the histories have gone untold for two years."

"Until now," Jesse pointed out.

"Until now."

Rae and Silas sat down on the bench to listen, but Jesse stood transfixed, as Noa pointed to each painting and described what happened in each.

When he reached the eighth painting, his story began to describe what led to the destruction of Urad. The scene was a cart full of uncut gems, pulled along a track by a Roaric miner while a Patrol member looked on.

"Of course, they mined for iron as well," Noa narrated. "But all of the materials went to the king, and our people were paid only a small portion of what they were worth."

The next painting showed five Roarics, four men and one woman, in front of a group of Patrol members. *Is that…Kasha?* The dwarves were, as the Roarics would say, Above-ground.

"My father and a few others decided to demand their rights. The Patrol members refused, and when my father threatened to incite the rest of the Roarics to a rebellion, they left in a fury. My father knew something terrible would happen, so he urged the people of Urad to leave the city. They would not, though he pleaded with them day after day. Then the army came."

The paintings became dark and ominous, filled with smoke and swords and death. Jesse could almost smell the burning buildings, hear the cries of the people, feel the panic that must have come with the Fall. "The king's retribution was swift, and nearly complete."

Here Noa paused, his face full of sadness. "Many—including my mother—were killed by the king's Patrol. Only a few escaped. My father was one of them. In the confusion, he ran with me to the mines, hiding in one of the shallow shafts that had not yet been fully drilled."

Jesse was drawn to that painting in particular. It showed a man huddled in little more than a deep ditch, shielding a small baby and looking upward in fear, as the gray boots of Patrol members ran by above them.

"Eventually, once the Patrol members were gone, the survivors found each other. Because remembering brought so much pain, the Roarics decided to forget—to forget what life had been like before, to forget the Fall, to forget their troubles, hoping that would make them disappear. My father refused to forget, and so he was called the History Keeper. After some time, the survivors built New Urad with the scraps the king's men had left behind."

Here Noa stopped. "But I hardly need to show you that painting. You have seen the city yourself. Life has changed very little over the past three decades." He walked away from the wall of paintings, shaking his head.

Then he looked up at them. "But I have talked too long. I have not yet asked you for your history. I doubt your story to the ruler clan was fully accurate." He looked at them expectantly.

Jesse was about to speak up, when Silas stood, motioning for him to be quiet. "Maybe not," he said firmly, "but it will have to stand for now."

Noa nodded, seeming to accept his answer, whether or not he understood it. "Would you like something to eat?" he offered. "I have only the small ration the hunter clan gives out, but…."

"No," Silas said quickly. "We have supplies of our own."

"But thank you," Jesse added.

"Perhaps something to drink, then?"

"Actually," Rae said, moving toward the door, "I have to say, I'm ready to leave. It's strange for us to be so far underground."

Noa nodded. "I understand, though it will be hard to say good-bye to my first—and perhaps only—guests. I will show you the way. It's not far from here."

"Wait," Silas said, stepping in front of him. He set his pack on the ground, and rummaged through it, pulling out the Rebellion symbol. Now, in the darkness, Jesse noticed what he had not before: the faint white glow around the stone. "What can you tell me about the Rebellion?"

"The Rebellion," Noa said softly, reaching out for the stone. "May I?"

At first, Silas jerked his hand back, studying Noa. "He's not going to steal it, Silas," Jesse said, exasperated.

"I know," Silas snapped. He handed the stone to Noa, who stared at the symbol carved into it.

"My father spoke of the Rebellion," he said. "In the old days, he was part of the represener clan, which dealt with the Above-grounders. The Patrol members hated the Rebellion, I remember that much."

"With good reason," Silas said bitterly.

Noa didn't seem to hear him. He stroked his chin thoughtfully. "There was one story my father used to tell. I remember it, because it was one of my favorites. He overheard a Patrol member talking one day, telling of a fellow Patrol who had gone mad and spoke of a place in the mines where there were traps and secret tunnels. He described it as 'the place where the fist pounds the mountain.'"

"The fist?" Rae asked, sounding confused.

"Yes, that's what the other Patrol member thought too. He described the man's ravings as a hilarious joke, and apparently thought nothing of them. My father thought differently. He knew of a place fitting the crazed Patrol's descriptions."

"How?" Jesse asked.

Noa shrugged. "Our people created these mines, nearly all of them. The first one was poorly planned, full of twists and turns and dead ends, deep in the heart of the mountains. It was mined of anything useful and abandoned generations ago. My father always believed that was the place the man spoke of."

"But what does that have to do with the Rebellion?" Silas pressed.

"Of course," Noa said, like he had forgotten. "The man also repeated the phrase, 'The Riddler's Pass. The riddler and the Rebellion.'" Noa smiled slightly. "My father told the story well, imitating the man's crazed words. But, though I found the story amusing, Riddler's Pass does not sound like a place hospitable to visitors."

A mild statement. "So their headquarters are somewhere in the Deep Mines," Jesse mused out loud.

"Yes," Noa agreed. "About half a day's journey from here, in fact, if I remember correctly."

"Then you know where the headquarters are?" Silas demanded, his voice rising in excitement. "Why didn't you tell us before?"

"You didn't ask before," Noa said, shrugging. "You asked what I could tell you about the Rebellion—its history. Its location is something to be looked up in a book of maps, not something to be told about. There is a difference."

"You have a book with a map of the Rebellion headquarters?" Silas asked in amazement.

Noa nodded. "The mountains are our home. You Above-grounders are newcomers here. In the old days, we had every ravine and crevice diagrammed. I am perhaps the only one who remembers."

"Why haven't you done anything with it? Told anyone?"

"Who would I tell?" Noa pointed out. "No one Above-ground knows we exist—besides you, of course. No one here cares. And besides, how do I know this Rebellion is evil?"

"They killed my father," Silas said in a dull, dead voice. "He was a priest, shot in an attempt by the Rebellion to murder the governor's steward. He was innocent—killed for no reason. What could be more evil than that? The king may do wrong, but it cannot compare to the evil of the Rebellion."

"Who are you to judge that?" Noa asked. "Is the evil that destroyed my mother and my people greater than the evil that destroyed your father?" His eyes, though squinting, seemed sharper as he stared at Silas.

Silas didn't answer. He just stared straight ahead, unblinking.

Without another word, Noa crossed over to the cluttered desk on the other side of the room and began rustling through papers and books. "I can't recall where it might be. Never added to it myself, you see."

Jesse sat back down on the ground to wait. Rae chose to pace, and Silas just stood, staring at Noa. "A map of the headquarters," he muttered to no one in particular. "And they had it all this time...."

"Here it is!" Noa said triumphantly, producing a thick volume. "*The Geography of the Suspicion Mountains.*" Silas was at his side immediately, and Jesse and Rae looked over Noa's shoulder, not a difficult task with a dwarf.

"Above-ground locations...." Noa muttered, his stubby finger running down a neat index. "Riddler's Pass." He looked up. "A label added by my father, of course." He turned the pages carefully and slowly. Silas tapped his foot in a repetitive beat on the floor.

Finally, Noa reached the right page. "There," he said, pointing. Spread out over both pages was the diagram of an elaborate tunnel system. Jesse could hardly follow all its twists and turns.

"A view from above," Noa explained. "This map is, of course, more than twenty-six years old, but perhaps it could be of use."

"Yes," Silas said, staring at the page. "Yes. This is what we've been waiting for."

Noa turned the page. "A wider view," he explained. Now the map showed the topography of the mountains themselves, and the nearby landmarks.

Silas took the book from Noa and pointed to a town near the border. "I know this village," he said. "Caven. My father was born there." He looked back at Jesse and Rae. "We can use this to get there," he said. "I know we can."

Something inside of Jesse wondered, *And then what?* But he said nothing.

Silas turned to Noa. "Can we take this with us?"

Noa just laughed. "A funny sight you would look on the road, hefting along a large volume of maps to find your way."

"I mean tear out the pages."

From the horrified look on Noa's face, Jesse would have guessed Silas had suggested killing his firstborn child. "Of course not." He snatched the book away from Silas. "I'll make a copy."

He took out a clean piece of parchment and dipped a quill in a half-full bottle of ink. "I don't have much left," he said apologetically. "It will have to be small."

"Just so we can read it," Jesse said, although Silas looked about to protest.

Several quick, fluid strokes later, Noa had outlined the features of the map. In surprisingly neat handwriting for someone with such clumsy-looking hands, he labeled the landmarks and added the necessary details.

Jesse admired the finished product. It wasn't an exact copy, but the lines were clear and accurate, though smaller. Noa clearly had an artist's eye.

"It will help," Silas said, studying the map again, then placing it carefully in his pack. "Do you think anyone else here will have more information?"

Noa laughed outright at that. "No. I know they will not. They discard any information that is not immediately useful for survival. The Roarics have always been a race of workers, not thinkers," he explained with a shrug. "And after the Fall, the leaders decided that it was the representer clan's questions and demands that caused the destruction of Urad. So questions, and with that curiosity and knowledge—became the enemy."

"Yet they have you, the History Keeper," Jesse pointed out.

"Yes, they have me," Noa said, giving a dry chuckle. "The village idiot, the strong young man who plays with heirlooms, paints on his walls, and writes records in books when he ought to be hunting and mining to ensure New Urad's survival."

Then he shook his head. "But this is no time to feel sorry for myself. I will lead you to the river."

The river?

But Noa continued without explaining. "I walk there often to get away from the town. It leads to a passage that will take you to the surface. Believe me, the other Roarics have already forgotten about you. You will not be missed." He paused. "At least, I hope not."

CHAPTER 6

They almost made it out of New Urad without any trouble. Noa was leading them all the way through the small village, when a dwarf with a pickaxe and a dark scowl stepped out from behind the last house. He stood firmly in their way, stocky arms crossed in an unspoken threat. Even though the Roaric was half his size, Jesse couldn't help feeling a little nervous.

"I don't suppose he's here to wish us good-bye," Jesse muttered.

"Doubt it," Noa muttered back. "Not Vane."

The Roaric, Vane, stepped forward. Dirt and sweat made lines on his wide forehead, making his sneer seem like something permanently etched into his face. "Going somewhere, History Boy?"

"Yes, I am," Noa said calmly, meeting his gaze. "To the river. To show the newcomers how to fish."

"So they can do work to help New Urad? Like you never do?"

"We all do our part, Vane. Now, step aside. Please."

Vane didn't seem to know how to respond to Noa's cool politeness. Jesse got the feeling this conversation had happened many times before.

Instead of moving, Vane looked up at the them. He stared longest at Rae. "You're a pretty little thing, for an Above-grounder," he said, grinning at her. "Maybe you're half Roaric yourself."

"Maybe," Rae said, her eyes blazing even in the dim light. "Like you, I'm small in frame. Unlike you, I'm not small of mind. That's half."

Vane's smile went away.

Jesse groaned inside. *Rae always knows how to make enemies.*

"Hold your peace, Vane," Noa said, as the other Roaric muttered angrily. "She's new here."

"She should go back where she belongs," Vane said, spitting at their feet. "All them should."

"I tried to tell Kasha that but she— "

"Not Above-ground," Vane growled. "In a grave."

With that he marched back into the pitiful streets of New Urad.

Noa watched him go. "Quickly," he said, "before he comes back and brings friends with him."

"He *has* friends?" Rae wondered out loud.

They hurried into the gash in the rock that led into a wide tunnel. The path was lined with the glowing stones, giving just enough light to see what was ahead.

"Friendly neighbors you have here," Jesse observed.

"Actually," Noa said, "I have more hope for him than the others."

"What do you mean?" Rae asked, shaking her head in disgust. "I'd like to smash his face in with one of these glowing rocks."

For a moment, Noa stared at her, as if bewildered that she could suggest such a thing. Then he said, "At least Vane cares. There is still some life in him. There are still some questions. He's come to all the wrong answers, of course. But at least he's asking."

That sounded crazy to Jesse, but Noa seemed to be a bit eccentric anyway. *Then again, after so many years alone in the dark, who wouldn't be?*

"What's that sound?" Silas asked, stopping.

Noa kept on going. "The river. We'll be coming to it soon."

Calling the trickling water a river was a bit of an exaggeration. Jesse decided it was more like a stream, especially compared to the strong, clear Dell River of his homeland. The thin band of water flowed along the path. Jesse prodded the water with his walking stick. In the middle, it would come only to his knees.

While Noa, Silas, and Rae walked on, Jesse stopped and took off his shoes. He had walked far over the last several days, and his lame leg was stiff and sore. At home, dipping it in cool water always helped. *I'll just walk in the river,* he reasoned. *I can still keep up.*

The bottom of the stream felt like gravel, but Jesse felt a sensation of relief as his leg dipped into the water with a small splash.

Noa must have heard, because he whirled around. "No!" he shouted, running toward Jesse. "Get out of there!"

No sooner had Jesse stepped back onto the rocky ground than the stream began to boil with movement. Jesse took another step backward, staring at the swirling water. He wondered at first if somehow he had triggered a whirlpool like he had heard of in sailors' stories. Then he saw tails and fins, pale in the dim light, sticking out of the water.

"Cave fish," Noa explained. "Jags and rockeyes, we call them. Blind as anything, with holes for eyes, but they can feel movement. They're carnivorous."

"You mean I could have..." Jesse sputtered. He took another few steps away. Even Silas looked a little startled at Noa's words.

"I've heard of a Roaric or two who lost a hand or foot that way," Noa said sadly, "often children too foolish to obey the warnings. But mostly, we're careful around them. They don't find many of our kind to eat."

Jesse jammed his feet back into his shoes, refusing to look at the fish again. Rae leaned a little closer to the water, which had calmed down some. "What do they eat, then?" she asked.

"Each other."

For the rest of the journey, all of them were careful to stay far away from the water. Jesse scraped his arm a few times on the far wall because he walked so close to it.

"They're very flavorful," Noa said, as if trying to persuade Jesse the fish weren't so bad after all. "As long as you pull off the scales first. They're as tough as armor."

Jesse shuddered. "I could never eat those...things."

"There isn't much food left," Noa said, shrugging. "We haven't gone Above-ground since the Fall, so our diet consists of fish and the animals that come into the mines that Roarics from the hunter clan kill."

So that's what Bern was doing so close to the surface, Jesse realized. Then he thought of something else. "No one will go to the entrance we came through," he said. "Not anymore."

Noa looked back at him. "What do you mean?"

Jesse explained about the cave-in, leaving out the details of why the king's men were chasing them. Noa didn't ask. "Another scene to add to the histories," he exclaimed. "And an exciting one, at that."

Jesse stared at him. "Aren't you afraid you'll run out of food, now that one of your passages is shut off?"

"Maybe it will force my people to leave," Noa said. "I've been trying to convince them for years, but now that Urad is gone forever, perhaps they will listen. Sometimes it's good to have every route taken away except the one that leads up to the light."

Secretly, Jesse wondered if anything would convince people like Kasha, Bern, and Vane to leave New Urad. *They'd rather die here, I think.*

After walking for a few more minutes, they found where the stream curved into a small crack in the stone wall, carrying the water to the caves and crags deeper in. "I must leave you here," Noa said.

Jesse looked around. No light shone from the surface as far as he could see. *And we haven't traveled up far enough. We must still be a long way underground.* "But how do we get Above-ground?"

"Continue straight on," Noa instructed. "The ground will begin to slope upward. I've only been past here once, as a boy. I remember many rock piles. Keep going, and you will see the entrance to the surface. All mines eventually lead there."

"Come with us," Jesse urged him. "You can't stay here forever."

"No," Noa said, shaking his head. "That would be the easy way—just as responding to the Fall by denying thought and questions was the easy way." He gestured to the dark cave. "And you can see where that leads."

Noa smiled, a tired, lonely smile. "But at least some good has come of this. I can now make the first new painting since Father died. He would have liked to meet you; I know it."

Rae was already backing down the tunnel. "Thank you for all you did for us."

"It was nothing," Noa said. "God go with you on your journey—wherever it might take you."

Jesse grunted. *Why does everyone keep saying that?* "I don't think God will be coming with us. If he exists at all, he probably hates me."

Noa cocked his head curiously. "And why do you say that?"

Jesse glanced down at his crippled leg. "Well, I can't walk well, for one. Where was God when the accident happened? Where was God when my parents disappeared? I didn't do anything to deserve it. Why do bad things happen to good people if God can stop them?"

"Ah," Noa said thoughtfully, apparently not bothered by Jesse's sharp words. "The Great Question. Put another way, why does a good, powerful God allow suffering? Jesse, if I knew the answer to that, I wouldn't believe in God; I would *be* God."

"Oh." Jesse didn't bother to hide the disappointment on his face. *Maybe the reason no one can answer the question is because there is no answer.*

"But," Noa continued, "perhaps I can share with you something I've learned. When I was young, I didn't understand why my father lived away from the rest of the village, or why he painted the Histories, or made what seemed to me to be strange, meaningless markings in his journal. But even though I didn't always know why, I trusted my father."

Noa reached up and put his hand on Jesse's shoulder, just like Jesse's father had once done. "And, to him, those strange markings made sense all along. Each fit together to form a greater story."

Jesse pictured the neat, clear letters on the worn pages of Noa's books. He couldn't think of anything to say.

"We really should go," Silas said. "You and your map have been of great help to us. I've waited for so long...." His voice trailed off, but there was a strange, new quality to it that Jesse didn't like.

Noa waved him on. "I understand. Above-grounders can't be kept in the darkness forever."

Silas and Rae continued into the darkness, but Jesse hesitated. *I'll come back someday*, he decided. *Then I'll tell Noa the adventures I have had with the Youth Guard.*

Before Jesse could say good-bye, Noa spoke up quietly. "It's destroying him."

Jesse blinked. "What?"

"Silas," Noa said. "Hatred is a form of evil. It can only destroy the person who holds it. Silas will have a hard time coming to the One who alone can conquer evil—harder than any of the rest of you—he wants too much to be in control."

What do I say to that? Jesse tried to make a joke. "So, the History Keeper is a prophet too?"

"No," Noa said, shaking his head, "but much of history is the study of people, and much of prophecy is the same. Sometimes a prophecy is just taking what is known from the past and applying it to the future. I was like him once."

That was difficult for Jesse to picture. The two seemed to be radically different. "Well, maybe there's hope for Silas after all," he said, half-joking. Noa's heavy tone was starting to worry him.

"You're right about that," Noa agreed. "There is always hope."

Jesse tried one last time. "Are you sure you won't join us?"

"Yes," Noa said, "but thank you. This is where God has placed me. When the Roarics decide to ask questions, to remember the past, and to learn from it, then they will have the courage to leave New Urad. But, until then, I must stay."

He stared into the dark, like he could see something far away. "I am the only light they have."

CHAPTER 7

"A slope upward, Noa said," Rae grunted, breathing heavily. "I would hardly call this a mere slope."

Jesse didn't answer, using all his energy to keep scrambling up each rock. This was the third pile they had climbed since leaving Noa. Along the way were a few of the steel carts they had seen at the other mines, and Jesse noticed for the first time the two parallel grooves that lined the tunnels.

For the wheels on the carts, he realized. *To haul gems and iron to the surface. We're going in the right direction, at least.* He wished they could climb in a cart and be hauled to the surface by a crew of Roarics, but the tracks were broken up by the huge piles of boulders Noa had warned them about.

Finally, at the top of the third rock heap, Jesse spotted the sight they had waited for: a pinprick of sunlight. Small though it was, the light gave Jesse the energy to continue.

This heap seemed to be steeper than the others, and Jesse had the sensation of climbing straight up a mountain cliff, although he knew it was no such thing. Rae, of course, was an excellent climber, but Silas lumbered behind Jesse, choosing the slower, but safer, routes.

Jesse stopped to rest, leaning against one of the cool stones. His body was soaked with sweat, and he was suddenly glad he had left his pack of supplies at the entrance to the cave. *I wouldn't have the strength to carry it now.*

Directly below him, Silas stopped too. "Here," he said, passing the water skin to Jesse. "Give it to Rae when you're done." Either he was too tired to ask where Jesse's own supplies were, or he didn't notice they were gone.

Jesse took a long gulp of water, cold and refreshing. "Catch," he called, tossing the water skin up to Rae. He didn't throw it far enough, and she had to duck down to grab it.

That sudden movement seemed to jar the boulder she was standing on. Jesse watched in horror as the boulder pulled away from the others, sending Rae tumbling down the pile.

Instinctively, he grabbed her as she fell, trying to steady her before she slid farther down the mountain of stones. Even though Rae had stopped, Silas was still shouting.

Jesse looked up to see several stones rolling down the pile. Rae's rock must have loosened others. Even as his mind processed that thought, he realized something more immediately important: *They're coming toward us!*

Instinctively, Jesse shoved Rae aside, toward Silas. At the same time, he leaped to the right, missing the boulder. *Get away!* his mind screamed, but there was nowhere to go without falling down the pile.

He saw a rock heading toward his head, but he had no time to move. A shooting pain raced jaggedly through him. Dimly, he heard his own voice crying out in pain.

Movement beside him. Voices. Jesse tried to focus enough to understand what Silas and Rae were saying, but he couldn't. It hurt too much.

Then, mercifully, black began to cloud his vision, and he didn't see or hear anymore.

When he opened his eyes again, his head still throbbed, but the sharp pain was gone. That was a relief.

He was Above-ground. The tree branch above him was a good sign of that. Jesse never realized how much he appreciated simple things like fresh air and the sun on his face.

"He's awake," Rae's voice said. Her dark eyes looked even wider than usual as she leaned down toward him.

"Are you all right?" Silas asked, joining her.

"Not yet, but I hope to be on my feet in no time," Jesse said dryly. Silas and Rae didn't smile. "Well, at least I have a hard head."

Still no reaction. Jesse gave up and focused on his injuries, reaching a hand up to touch his head. Even through the bandages, he could feel the lump on his temple. "One of our blankets is torn up now, I assume," he said.

Silas shook his head. "Part of the tent. The canvas was thicker."

"You were bleeding a lot," Rae added. She didn't exactly sound concerned, but she hadn't left him underground to die. That was something.

"It must have been the rubble from old mine shafts," Jesse said, his voice not quite steady. "No wonder the rocks were loose—there was nothing to hold them together."

"I was surprised you didn't get crushed," Rae said bluntly. "You should consider yourself lucky."

"How did I get here?" Jesse asked, glancing around.

"We carried you," Silas said.

Jesse frowned. "You shouldn't have done that. You could have fallen."

"It was either that or leave you behind," Rae pointed out, sitting down on the grass. "Stop being so noble."

"I'm not being noble," Jesse protested. "If you were carrying me, I would have fallen with you."

Silas turned to Rae. "I liked him better when he was unconscious."

Even though his leg throbbed with pain, Jesse smiled a little. "Where are we?"

"Just outside the cave," Silas said. "We found a grove of trees nearby. We'll spend the night here."

"Can you move?" Rae asked.

"I think so." Jesse stretched a little, then sat up slowly, leaning against the tree. Now he could see the mountains through the trees. There was a small hole in the rock near the ground. "You crawled through that?" he asked, amazed.

Rae nodded. "Silas wanted to pull aside more boulders to make it larger, but I told him that was foolish. If we accidentally loosened the rocks beneath us, we would be at the bottom of the pile again—if we managed to live."

"She had to pull me out of the opening," Silas said, rubbing his shoulder. Suddenly, Jesse wished he had been awake for that part. *It would have been very entertaining.*

Rae stood and walked over to a pine on the other side

of their camp. When she came back, she was holding Jesse's walking stick.

"Here," she said, handing it to him. "I dug it out of the rocks. Silas wanted to leave it behind, but I told him that you'd try to crawl back into the cave to get it."

"You're probably right," Jesse said, gripping the familiar wood of the staff. "Thank you."

Then he glanced at his leg, the crippled left one. It, too, was wrapped in a bandage.

Silas followed his gaze. "Another rock grazed you before I got there," he said. "Just tore the skin up, mostly. You should be able to walk just fine. As well as usual, I mean," he added quickly.

Jesse tried to be cheerful. "Well, at least it was the one that was already mangled."

"What happened to your leg?" Rae asked, staring at it.

"Hmm?" Jesse said, jerking his head up. He grinned a little. "Oh, a rock fell on it."

"No, I mean before that," Rae said, rolling her eyes. "If you don't mind saying," she added quickly.

Jesse shook his head. "I don't mind. It was five years ago, when I was ten. I was playing with a friend of mine in the village stables. We were teasing one of the horses, a beautiful, spirited chestnut stallion."

Understanding flickered across Rae's face. "Oh," she said. As one who knew much about horses, she could clearly see where this story was going.

Jesse continued anyway. "My friend, Eli, dared me to jump on its back. I had been riding often before, and I

73

thought I could handle this new horse. I was wrong. It wasn't used to a strange rider, I suppose, and it was already annoyed. Whatever the reason, it began to buck furiously, throwing me to the ground. I tried to roll away, but it stomped on my leg several times."

He closed his eyes, remembering the pain he had felt then, much stronger than what he felt even now. "If my father hadn't come running, I might have been trampled to death."

"It must have been a hard loss, the use of your leg, I mean," Silas said.

"Accidents happen," Jesse said, shrugging. "If anyone was to blame, I was, for being so foolish. Besides, I get along well enough. My limp taught me a lesson. I just wish I didn't have to learn it the hard way."

His words were optimistic, as they always were when someone asked him about his crippled leg. They were true enough. But although the pain of the accident soon died away, Jesse could still remember the greater pain—not being able to participate in the harvest time footraces, trying to ignore the stares and whispers of pity when he went into town, hearing the other children laugh at him.

Not that they did that often, he remembered with a bit of a smile. *Not while Eli was around, anyway.* Eli had always been his defender after the accident, and now Jesse wondered again what was happening to him. *I hope his mission is going better than ours.*

The sun was just starting to set, and although Jesse knew it had only been a few hours since he had slept at the mouth of the cave, he felt exhausted again.

"Well," Jesse said, "I suppose it's time to go to sleep."

"Yes," Silas said. "We'll need to move on tomorrow."

"So soon?" Jesse asked doubtfully. Sure, his head seemed to be all right, but it would be nice to rest for a while.

Silas frowned at him in surprise. "Of course."

"But, Silas," Rae said, "he has to have time to heal. Can't we wait a day or two?" Although it surprised him, Jesse had to admit it was nice to have Rae defending him for a change.

"We'll travel slowly," Silas promised, "but we have to go forward. Think of Parvel and the danger he is in."

Interesting. He didn't seem terribly concerned about rushing into Mir to find Parvel just two nights ago. But Jesse could see that Silas had made up his mind. *Then we break camp in the morning.* The thought made Jesse even more tired. "And where, exactly, are we going?"

"Riddler's Pass," Silas said firmly. He pulled his blanket from his pack and spread it on the ground.

"And once we get there, what will we do?" Rae asked.

"I don't know."

Of course not. "We shouldn't forget that Bern made us leave our weapons in the cave," Jesse pointed out, "which is now completely collapsed."

Silas just stared at him, as if waiting for Jesse to get to the point. Jesse sighed. "Silas, you can't possibly expect us to storm the hiding place of the most ruthless faction of the Rebellion unarmed! What do you plan to do—throw rocks at them?"

"We aren't entirely unarmed," Silas said. He reached into his pack and pulled out two small sheaths. "We have

Rae's dagger and the dagger Samar gave me before we left him in the desert camp."

"You mean you had those all along, down in New Urad, and you didn't use them?" Rae blurted.

"What purpose would that have served?" Silas asked. "If I had felt we were in immediate danger, I would have taken them out. But we never were, so I never did."

Cautious, as usual, Jesse thought. *Then why is Silas so determined to take the foolish, risky way when it comes to Riddler's Pass?*

Of course, he knew the answer. The Rebellion killed Silas' father, and he wanted revenge. Even Noa had noticed that.

Silas stood. "You and Rae sleep. I'll keep watch."

"I still don't think…" Jesse began.

But Silas had already paced away to the edge of the grove of trees.

"Leave it," Rae advised, retreating to one of the tents. "He's clearly made up his mind."

But, try as he might, Jesse could not just leave it. Slowly, leaning on his staff and ignoring the twinge of pain, he stood and limped over to Silas. "I said I would take first watch," Silas said, hearing him approach.

"It's not that. I…." Jesse paused, trying to think of what to say. "You don't seem yourself lately." Silence. "Well, not lately, really, just…just when you talk about the Rebellion."

"I have my reasons," Silas said.

Jesse could see Silas' face clearly in the moonlight, and, without thinking, he shivered. Something was terribly wrong. Oh, the pale blond hair hadn't changed. Neither had the sharp nose and strong chin. It was his eyes. Pale gray in the moonlight, they stared into the darkness with a look of pure hatred Jesse had never seen before, and certainly hadn't seen in Silas before.

"Oh," Jesse said at last. He couldn't think of anything to say. *There's no use in talking to him now.*

"Goodnight, then," he said, limping back to the tent. Although he had a nagging feeling he had given up too soon, it was easier than trying to talk to someone who didn't want to listen. Maybe in the morning he would try again. Jesse yawned and closed his eyes. *Yes. In the morning.*

Jesse awoke to a hand clamped firmly over his mouth. He drew a breath to cry out for help, when he heard Silas whisper. "Not a word, Jesse."

What's happening? It couldn't be time for them to break camp; it was still dark.

Then another voice, a distant one Jesse didn't recognize. "He's cocky, that's what he is. Bossy too. Comes in from District Four, orders us to follow him, and now he keeps us trapped in the mountains. Who does he think he is, anyway? That's what I want to know."

"Just be quiet and look around," another voice replied.

As Jesse's eyes adjusted to the dark, his tired mind realized what was happening. *Captain Demetri's Patrol—they're still here! And just beyond the trees.*

Silas removed his hand, satisfied Jesse wouldn't betray their presence with a shout. Rae was behind Silas, and both stared past the trees toward the mountain, tensed and ready to flee at any moment.

"They couldn't possibly have lived through the cave-in," the first one continued, in a whining, nasal voice. "We barely got out alive. Even if they didn't get crushed right away, they'll be trapped."

Jesse shivered, picturing the slow end he could have met, pinned under a boulder, starving but unable to die.

"The captain says to check the perimeter once every watch," the other replied patiently. "We do it. At least, we pretend to. An easy assignment—we'll be back home in a few days once the captain is satisfied."

His eyes wide, Jesse tried not to breathe. *Will they see us in the trees?*

"Look at this," the nasal Patrol member said, laughing. "Not a rock out of place. Those children are as good as gone. Don't know what all the fuss is about anyhow. Come on, let's get back to the western side. Likely the others will have eaten all the rations without us."

Two sets of footsteps, one of them sounding like they were kicking small stones, clunked into the night. For the first time in his life, Jesse was glad the lazy and dishonest often filled the ranks of the king's Patrol.

"What are we going to do?" he whispered, after he was sure the Patrol members were gone.

"We will leave. Tonight," Silas said grimly. "That is, if you can walk, Jesse."

"Why?" Jesse asked. "They don't know we're here."

"They could find us," Silas said. "Or see traces of our camp. Matted grass, displaced stone. We can't assume all the Patrol are as careless as those two. Never underestimate your enemy."

It sounded sensible when he put it that way, but Jesse suspected Silas really just wanted to get to the headquarters as soon as possible. With the Rebellion in sight, sleep wasn't important to him anymore.

Jesse picked up his walking stick from the ground beside him. Rae offered him her hand, but he waved it away and tried to stand on his own. His head throbbed a little, but the dizziness was gone. "I won't be able to move as quickly as I did before," he admitted.

"Never mind," Silas said. "The main thing is getting away from here. It sounds like the Patrol will be camped here for a while."

Making sure we're dead. The thought chilled Jesse, more than the cool mountain air, and gave him enough motivation to pack the supplies, cover up all traces of their camp, and leave the grove of trees behind.

"I didn't want any sleep tonight anyway," Jesse muttered to himself. He knew it was a lie, but it didn't matter. If Silas said to move on, they would move on until they reached Riddler's Pass. After that who knew what they would find?

Jesse remembered Noa's story about the Patrol member who went mad, and he wasn't sure he wanted to find out.

CHAPTER 8

Jesse began to hate traveling in the mountains even more than he had hated the desert. Besides being exhausting, the travel was dull and tedious. Every path looked the same, and even the mountains seemed like taller or shorter versions of the same exact rocks. Jesse found himself hoping the Rebellion headquarters were nearby. *At least then we could stop and rest.*

He hoped so, anyway. With Silas' current state, it was hard to say for sure.

They walked all through what was left of the night, until the sky got lighter and the air warmer as dawn approached. Every few minutes, Silas would pull out Noa's map and glance around at their surroundings.

Once, Jesse heard Silas muttering to himself as he walked

"What are you doing?" Jesse asked.

Silas didn't even stop. "Counting paces," he said. "That way I know the distance."

It made sense to Jesse. Silas always thought of everything.

Except, of course, that a wounded cripple would have a difficult time walking quickly. It was all Jesse could do to keep up with Silas. Despite what he said about traveling slowly, Silas pushed them ahead. They even ate while they walked.

We're supposed to be rescuing Parvel from the Rebellion, not following Silas' quest for revenge. Jesse almost said it, almost asked Silas if he had forgotten the purpose of their mission. Then he decided that would only make Silas angry. "How much farther?" Jesse asked instead.

"We should reach Riddler's Pass soon, if this map is accurate," Silas said.

Jesse was glad to hear it. He had never been so sore, not even after traveling through the desert. His leg was throbbing with pain, but he kept going. Silas would probably leave him behind if he slowed.

For a while, he counted his own paces, more to keep his mind off the pain in his leg than to track how far they had walked. Suddenly, right before Jesse reached a thousand paces, Silas stopped in the middle of the path, staring into the sky.

"There it is," he said, pointing to the east in awe. "The fist pounding the mountain. Just where the map said it would be."

Sure enough, the rising sun just beyond the mountains showed a clear silhouette of a rock formation stacked on top of a plateau. It truly did look like a fist, with four boulder knuckles and a rounded rock thumb jutting out of the hand. *It would only be clearly visible in the dawn light*, Jesse realized. *Otherwise, it would blend in with the rocks behind it in the distance.*

Rae and Silas immediately ran toward the cliff face. Jesse limped along at his own slow pace.

By the time he got there, Rae and Silas were studying the rock wall of the canyon beneath the fist, looking puzzled. It was small, perhaps only thirty paces deep and seven paces wide.

"I don't see anything," Rae said at last, running her hands over the stone. "Not an opening, not a cave, and certainly not a pass."

Jesse looked around. No patches of briars could cover up a secret entrance, no tiny crevice in the rock could be seen for them to squeeze through. "Maybe we got the wrong fist."

"It has to be here!" Silas exclaimed in frustration, pacing back and forth beside the canyon wall. "It has to be. It looks just like the canyon on the map."

"Maybe the map was wrong," Jesse suggested. "It was an old map. Besides, the Roarics didn't go Above-ground much. Things could have changed."

"We'll look closer," Rae said, giving Jesse a warning look. "It will make him feel better, at least," she whispered to him as she passed.

Fine. I'll waste my time in a boxed-in canyon to make Silas feel better. Jesse kicked the mountain to see if anything moved. He only succeeded in hurting his good foot.

On the other side of the canyon, Rae and Silas were feeling the rock. "Maybe you'll find some sort of trap door," Jesse suggested, grinning. "Or a hidden lever that will pry the mountains apart. Or a magic portal that will take you to the Rebellion lair."

Both glared at his attempt at humor and continued their careful search.

So he would at least look like he was searching, Jesse tapped his staff against the rocks, first lightly, then harder. After a while, he began to beat out a rhythm, the solid *tap, tap, tap* of the stick against stone creating a pattern of sound. *This is actually fun.*

He began to step in time to the rhythm, like the people of Mir did at the annual harvest celebration. With one swollen, lame leg, it was a sad imitation, to be sure, but it was better than poking at Silas' barren mountain.

Jesse danced up the length of the canyon, tapping the rock all the way. Then, right before he reached the dead end, his good foot tripped on something, and he sprawled to the ground—hard. Strangely, the dirt and moss underneath him shuddered slightly.

"Are you all right?" Silas called, looking up from his work at the noise of Jesse's fall.

"Just fine," Jesse said, not wanting to explain what had happened. When Silas and Rae turned back to their search, Jesse looked down. *That's strange.* Beneath him was a large patch of dead moss among all the green.

Maybe it's some sort of fungus or disease. The thought made him pull away, and he scurried over to the green moss nearby. *What did I trip over, anyway?*

He peered into the square of dead moss and saw it, nearly buried in the ground. An iron ring. *Someone left it here, I suppose. Maybe the metal poisoned the moss around it.*

Jesse reached down to pick it up, but it would not budge. *It's attached*, he realized. Then, another thought immediately after it: *What if this moss isn't poisoned or diseased? What if it's a patch of dead moss that was used to cover up something…like a door?* "Silas," he called, excited now. "Come over here!"

Silas and Rae both came, although neither one seemed to be in much of a hurry. "What is it?" Silas asked. "Do you need help standing back up?"

Jesse gave him a scathing look. "No. But look what I found."

He pointed to the iron ring in the moss, and Silas seemed to understand right away. "A secret entrance," he breathed, staring at it. "Noa's map was right after all."

"We don't know that for sure until we try," Rae pointed out. "It could be locked. Or the place could be abandoned."

"Then let's try," Silas said, grasping the ring.

The first pull yielded nothing. "It's locked," Silas groaned, his face twisted in frustration.

"No," Rae said, shaking her head, "I saw the ground move. Try again."

This time, Silas used both hands, his muscles straining to pull the door open. Something in the ground seemed to give way, and a thick square of turf and moss pulled away. Jesse could now see that the slab was attached to a wooden panel that opened to reveal a black gash in the ground.

They surrounded the hole, looking into it. "How do we get down?" Jesse wondered out loud. "I hope not by jumping."

In response, Rae reached into the hole and pulled up the first few rungs of a rope ladder. "We climb."

"I'm still not sure this is a good idea," Jesse said. "Noa spoke of traps and pitfalls. You and Silas are armed only with small daggers. Maybe we should go to a town nearby and get more supplies."

"The nearest town is almost a day's travel away," Silas said. "I cannot—will not—wait that long."

Jesse sighed, knowing any further arguments would be useless. *I liked the old Silas better.*

Silas stared into the hole. "I'll give those Rebellion cowards their just punishment."

"And rescue Parvel," Jesse reminded him.

"Of course," Silas said, as if that was something so obvious he hadn't felt the need to mention it. He pointed to the pit. "Now, come on."

Knowing he wouldn't be able to climb while holding his staff, Jesse dropped it into the hole. A split second later, it hit the ground with a dull thud.

"Do you want to announce our presence?" Silas demanded, grabbing Jesse by the shoulders and shaking him. "What if someone heard?"

"I'm sorry," was all Jesse could manage. "I didn't think."

Silas never looked away. "Well, start thinking. No one will ruin this mission. Understand?"

"Silas," Rae warned.

He glanced at her, then released his grip on Jesse's shoulders, looking a little ashamed.

"Well, let's go," Rae said, staring at the hole. "No turning back now. After all, Jesse, you have to get your stick back."

"After you, Silas," Jesse offered generously. *I don't care if they think I'm a coward; I will not be the first to descend into the pit.*

Silas shook his head. "I'll replace the door," he said. "It's too heavy for either of you."

That earned him a glare from Rae, who led the way into the hole.

Jesse was squarely in the middle. *Not a bad place to be*, he mused as he stepped onto the rope ladder. *Rae can catch me if I fall. Silas can pull me to the surface if the rope ladder breaks.*

But the rope did not break, though Silas tested it with his quick, jerking movements. "Slow down," Jesse muttered, as one of Silas' hurried steps swung the rope ladder forward, nearly bashing his nose into the wall.

Jesse frowned as he jumped down from the rope ladder. *Another tunnel.* This time, though, they were surrounded by hard-packed dirt instead of stone. *So that's why my staff didn't clatter when it hit the ground.*

Jesse began feeling around for his staff, when suddenly a glow pushed away the dark. Jesse glanced over to see that Silas had the Rebellion stone out again. Jesse took advantage of the light to find his staff, then caught up with Silas and Rae.

Soon, the dirt ended, and the walls of the tunnel turned to stone. "We're inside the mountain," Rae said, almost in awe, as they stepped into a large cavern.

But Silas was no longer listening to her. He was staring at the far end of the cavern.

Jesse followed his gaze, and his jaw dropped open.

It was a wall of glowing stones like the one in Noa's house, only much larger. Right next to it were twin pillars of stone, framing another gaping hole.

"There's something carved on the wall," Rae said, sounding excited.

She was right. In large letters at the top of the wall that could be seen even from a distance were these words:

> HERE IN THE STONE ARE RIDDLES THREE;
> SYMBOLS OF YOUR DESTINY.
> THOSE WHO SOLVE THEM SOON WILL FIND
> THE KEY FOR ENTRANCE IS THE MIND.

"Riddler's Pass," Silas said, nodding. "It makes sense. The riddle must be some sort of key for navigating the tunnels."

"Navigating?" Rae asked.

Silas nodded and pulled out Noa's map. "Look at this." Jesse looked at it more carefully than he had in New Urad. It was almost like a maze in its complexity. "They have the tunnels drawn," Silas said, "but not labeled in any way."

"So the map is useless," Rae summarized. Silas nodded. "I hate riddles," she muttered to herself.

Jesse had already limped closer to the stone. There, carved in smaller letters, were three blocks of text, spaced along the middle portion of the wall. Each letter was crisp and well-formed. *So they are recent*, Jesse decided. *Although, with no wind to beat at them, who knows if that's true?*

"Read the first aloud," Silas instructed Jesse.

Jesse did. The letters, though bold, were hard to see in the glowing stone.

To own it you must win it, and risk a world of ache.
Your quest to steal this treasure
may cause your own to break.

There was silence in the cavern for a few moments. "'Your own,'" Jesse said out loud. "If you already have one, why do you need to steal another?"

"I don't know!" Silas groaned. "I wish Parvel was here. He was always good at mind games."

They stared at the rock, as if the answer would suddenly appear. "And if you have to win it to own it," Rae said thoughtfully, "then how can you steal it?"

It was a good point, but not a very helpful one. Jesse felt even more confused.

"Maybe trying to steal it doesn't work," Silas offered. "It said that something will break if you try."

That's it. "It's a heart," Jesse said. Rae looked at him blankly. "To win someone's heart, you must risk ache," Jesse explained. "And your heart may even break if you try to steal another's heart and are rejected."

"It must be the answer," Silas agreed. "Good work, Jesse."

Jesse tried not to grin with pride. It didn't work well. "Here is the next one," he said, taking a step to the right.

Within me there is life and hope,
far from the fish and fin.
My walls of stone are strong and thick,
but see no battle din.
I do not keep out friend or foe, but keep my contents in.

"A prison," Rae said immediately. "It keeps something in."

"True," Jesse acknowledged, "but what about the first part?"

Rae shrugged. All of them had been in a prison, back in Da'armos, and Jesse knew it was not the place to go to find life and hope.

"No, no," Silas said, staring at the riddle. "I wonder…."

"And aren't fish and fin the same thing?" Jesse interrupted. "Why did they need to repeat it?"

Silas nodded. "'Far from the fish and fin'—far from the river, perhaps. And the life and hope of the river…water. But what about the walls?"

"So a prison with no water," Rae suggested. "Maybe the moat around it is dry."

Jesse shook his head at her, the last detail of the riddle falling into place. "Think about it," he said. "Something made of stone that keeps in water."

"A well," Rae said, finally understanding.

"Yes," Jesse agreed. "A well."

"Only one more," Silas said, sounding satisfied. He paced toward the stone pillars and glanced back impatiently. "Let's finish these so we can go on."

Jesse shrugged and read the third riddle.

I AM THE WEAKER BROTHER.
WHEN I AM NEW, I'M NOT.
MY REIGN IN HALF DIVIDED.
THE DARK IS WHAT I GOT.

"It talks about a reign," Rae mused. "A king of some kind?"

Jesse glanced over at Silas. This time, he was not staring at the rock with a distant, thoughtful expression. Instead, he was grinning like a fool. "Not a king," Silas corrected, "a governor."

"A governor?" Jesse asked. He knew, of course, that each of the four districts in Amarias was ruled under a governor, a regent of the king. But that alone did not make sense of the riddle. "Explain."

"Only someone who lives in District Two would understand it," Silas said. "That's why it's perfect for a riddle guarding the District Two Rebellion base. No outsider would be able to solve it."

Jesse glanced at Rae, who seemed to be equally exasperated. "I wouldn't call that an explanation, Silas," she said.

"Governor Patrice," Silas said. "Eight years ago, he tried to take over the throne from his brother. He succeeded, but only reigned for two years before he was assassinated."

"I see," Rae said. "And what does that have to do with the riddle?"

"Patrice was weaker than his brother Mirad," Silas explained patiently. "When he was born—new—he was not king. His reign was divided by the rebels who assassinated him. And darkness, death, was what he got."

"That does make sense," Rae admitted.

Does it really? "But then why doesn't it say, 'When I was new, I wasn't,' instead of 'When I am new, I'm not?'" Jesse pointed out.

Rae looked at him like his mind was made of rock. "Because it wouldn't rhyme."

"Oh." Jesse looked at the riddle again. "But what about 'my reign in half divided'? Did Patrice intend on ruling only—four years?"

"Maybe he was cut in half!" Rae guessed.

Jesse tried not to picture that and Silas shook his head. "No. As I recall, he was stabbed by the governor who is ruling now, Elias." He turned to Jesse. "It's just an expression, anyway. It means his reign was cut short."

Jesse sighed. He traced the letters of the riddle with his finger. "I don't know...."

"Just because you didn't solve this one doesn't mean you have to find problems with Silas' solution," Rae said.

"That's not what I meant!" Jesse protested.

"Never mind," Silas interrupted. "We have more important things to worry about. Come on." He gestured toward the gaping hole beside the wall of riddles. Jesse stared down it. *More tunnels.* "They must lead to the Rebellion headquarters." He and Rae began to walk into the darkness with only the Rebellion stone to light their way.

"But what was the purpose of the riddles?" Jesse asked, trying to catch up.

"The main rhyme says, 'The key for entrance is the mind,'" Silas said. "Maybe the riddles are a password of some sort." He touched the dagger, in a sheath at his side. "Whatever happens, I will be ready."

CHAPTER 9

Jesse remembered when the only time he was surrounded by darkness was at night, right before he went to sleep. *Was that only a month ago?* It seemed like it had been years. Now, entering a dark tunnel lit by eerie glowing stones actually seemed normal.

"When we find Parvel and get out of here," Jesse muttered, "I never want to go underground again."

"Don't be so afraid," Silas scoffed. "We haven't seen a guard or any sign of danger."

"That's what makes me nervous," Jesse said. "If this is the stronghold of the cunning, powerful Rebellion you always talk about, why isn't it guarded?"

"Maybe the traps Noa spoke of are enough to guard it," Rae offered. She began to walk a bit slower, glancing down at the ground. "We should be careful."

Yes, the traps. That was another problem. "I have a feeling these tunnels were designed so only those of the Rebellion, who know of the traps, will be able to survive."

Usually, it would have been Silas who thought of that,

who would have insisted on going no further until they were sure of what they would find. *But not now, not when he is so driven by revenge he ignores common sense.*

Sure enough, Silas only reacted to his comment with a shrug. "The Patrol member Noa told us about survived, didn't he?"

Silas must have missed the point of the story. As Jesse remembered it, the guard had been driven mad, raving about all kinds of terrors.

Jesse stepped forward, next to Rae. "Can't you say something to him?" he whispered to her. "Maybe he'll listen to you." She just looked at him blankly, her face even paler than normal in the light of the glowing stones. "Don't you agree that this is foolish?"

Rae paused, tucking a strand of black hair behind her ear. "Maybe," she said at last. "But we have to find Parvel. This seems like it's the only way to do that." She looked up at Silas, who had not stopped with them. "And I doubt anything either of us say will be able to convince Silas. He's beyond that now."

As he walked deeper into the tunnel, Jesse decided he now knew what it must feel like to be a donkey, bucking against the pull of a rope that would take him where he did not want to go. *But it's my choice,* he reminded himself. *I could turn back.*

And go back alone, leaving my friends behind. Jesse sighed and kept walking. *Maybe I don't have a choice after all.*

They had only walked into the tunnel a few paces when the path in front of them split in two.

Jesse asked the question they were all thinking. "Which way?"

Rae walked between the two archways. She bit her lip and turned around. "The one on the left looks deeper. I can't see very far, but it looks like the right leads to a dead end."

"Let me see." Silas squinted down both tunnels. "We'll take the left then."

Without waiting for agreement, he plunged through the left archway. Rae followed, hand on her dagger and eyes darting back.

Jesse pulled back, still not convinced. There were no cries of alarm from the archway on the left.

"There's a walkway covered with straw," Rae's voice echoed back to him. "This must be it!"

Jesse glanced again at the archways. The few glowing stones nearby did not provide enough light to see down either tunnel. One of the stones, placed above the right archway, the one Silas had not chosen, caught Jesse's eye.

"Come on, Jesse." Silas' voice, from the tunnel on the left.

Something's carved in it, he thought, taking a step forward toward the stone above the right archway.

It was a heart.

Jesse's own heart began to beat faster as he realized their mistake. "Silas!" he shouted, whirling around toward the other passageway. "Come back! We have to…."

But his words were cut off with two nearly identical sounds: a deep shout and a piercing scream. *Silas and Rae!*

In the second it took Jesse to run through the archway,

he saw Silas, breathing hard, lying on a ledge. Seeing the blackness, Jesse felt sick. *Where is Rae?*

"Help!" her voice cried. Jesse leaned over the side of the drop-off to see Rae, her hands clawing at an outcropping and her legs dangling into a black abyss. She was just out of reach.

"The rope," Silas shouted at Jesse. "Get the rope!"

His fingers shook as he undid Silas' pack, trying to dig through their supplies. "Here!"

Jesse passed it to Silas, who dropped it to Rae, bracing himself to pull her up. For a second, she just stared at it. Jesse knew what she must be thinking. *How can she risk letting go?*

Then Rae's hand slipped slightly. With a sharp gasp, she let go of the rock ledge with her right hand and gripped the rope. Her left hand followed, and she clung to the rope, her eyes tightly closed.

Silas began to pull, the muscles on his lean frame stretching as he brought the rope up, knot by knot. As soon as Rae's shoulders appeared, Jesse knelt to help her up. She scrambled onto the rock, moving as far from the edge as possible.

As his heart returned to its normal pace, Jesse stared out at the gorge. All that was left of the straw was a pile at the bottom of the cliff. Dimly, Jesse could see the glinting metal of spikes buried in the ground.

"I think," Rae said at last, a slight tremble giving away the fear in her voice, "we picked the wrong way."

"They spread the straw over a cloth," Silas said, shaking his head. "It couldn't hold our weight." He shuddered, looking down at the spikes. "I had only taken one step. Any farther, and I wouldn't have been able to jump to safety."

"We can't do this," Rae said. "Who knows how many more tunnels there will be? We'll die before we reach the headquarters."

"Not necessarily," Jesse said. In the dark, he knew they could not see him smile, but he did anyway. "What if I told you I know a way to choose the correct tunnel every time?"

"I would be interested," Silas said, eying him carefully. "Skeptical, but interested."

Jesse led them back into the tunnel, then turned so he was facing the two archways. "See?" he said, pointing to the glowing stone above the second path. "A heart."

"Just like in the riddle," Rae said. She stepped closer and fingered its rough curve.

Now Jesse could see several symbols, each one carved into a glowing stone set above both archways. "'Symbols of your destiny,'" he quoted. "The riddles mark which passage we should take."

Silas studied the archway. "But there are other symbols above this one besides a heart," he said. "A fish, a bow, a bird. Why are they there?"

Jesse shrugged. "To confuse people, I guess. Or maybe they're important for some other reason. But I don't think it's a coincidence that the right path happens to be marked with the symbol of the first riddle."

Sure enough, when the path split again, Rae found the symbol they were looking for, again on the right. "Here," she said, pointing to a stone at eye level in the archway. "Three rows of three small circles, stacked on top of each other. *The stones of a well.*

The first few steps into the new tunnel were the hardest, even though Jesse was sure his theory was right. *No pits of snakes, raging beasts, or pots of boiling oil so far.*

"Pots of boiling oil?" Rae questioned, turning back to him.

Jesse felt his face turn red as he realized he had been muttering to himself. "Well, it's possible," he said, defensively. Rae just laughed and continued into the dark tunnel.

Finally, the tunnel curved, then split again. Two more archways. They spread out and examined the symbols around the tunnels.

"What exactly are we looking for?" Jesse asked, running his hands over the designs carved into the rocks by the left tunnel. "Did Governor Patrice have a symbol?"

"Not that I know of," Silas said. "Just look for something that symbolizes royalty or leadership." A pause. "Like this!"

Rae and Jesse joined him, as he pointed to a diamond symbol near the ground. "You see? Diamonds are a symbol of royalty."

"But all of the others had a picture of the actual answer to the riddle," Jesse pointed out. "How do we know this is the right symbol?" He paused. "More importantly, what will happen if it isn't?"

"You're thinking too hard," Silas said dismissively. "It has to be the diamond."

Jesse took a deep breath. "No," he said, grabbing Silas by the shoulder. "It's not right."

"How do you know?" Silas asked impatiently, pulling away.

"It doesn't feel right," Jesse said lamely, unable to find a better explanation.

"Well, you and your feelings can be wrong, you know," Silas shot back. "What do you want us to do: sit here and stare at the two tunnels all day?"

"Silas," Rae scolded, "he's only trying to help. And I think he may be right."

"Fine," Silas said, folding his arms. "Then what are we going to do?"

"Well," Rae said, looking at the other archway, "do any of these symbols fit the riddle? What was it again?"

Jesse sat down in front of the left tunnel. "I am the weaker brother," he recited wearily. "When I am new, I'm not. My reign in half divided. The dark is what I got."

The darkness. What could you divide and have half be darkness?

Then Jesse thought of it. *Day and night.* "It's day and night," he said.

"That's not a symbol either," Silas pointed out.

"No, not the answer to the riddle," Jesse said, shaking his head. "Just part of it." He ran through the rhyme again in his mind. "The moon," he said. "It has to be the moon! The sun and moon are brothers...."

"...and the moon is weaker," Rae finished, nodding. "And you can't see a new moon, so when it's new, it's like it isn't there at all."

"Right," Jesse said, "and the moon reigns in the darkness—half of a full day."

Rae pointed to a carving in the left archway. It was a simple circle. "Look, a full moon." From where he was seated, it was at Jesse's eye level—*right in front of me!*

"It makes sense," Silas admitted. "But what if the answer really is Governor Patrice? Or what if the circle doesn't represent a full moon at all?"

For a moment, Jesse paused, staring into the dark to consider Silas' words. Then he noticed something: a thin wire stretched a few steps inside the diamond tunnel. *I never would have seen it if I hadn't been looking for something.* "Stand back," he said, pushing Rae and Silas aside. Then, staying clear of the entrance, he edged his staff toward the wire.

As soon as the staff touched the wire, Jesse heard a sharp clicking noise. Five arrows shot out of the dark with blurring speed, bouncing off the far wall and clattering to the ground.

Silas stepped forward, his dagger drawn. "Show yourself," he demanded of the attackers in the cave.

Jesse commanded himself not to laugh. "Silas, the arrows were just a trap. Probably crossbows rigged to fire when someone tightened the wire by stepping on it."

Rae shivered, staring at the fallen arrows. "You mean that would have been us?" Jesse nodded, and she turned to the remaining passageway. "I think I'll choose Jesse and the moon."

Silas grunted, but led the way into the left tunnel. "This was the last riddle," Jesse reminded them in a whisper. "We should reach the entrance to the hideout soon."

The doubts and misgivings Jesse had felt at the entrance of the cave grew until they were like voices shouting in his head. "Maybe we should send one person in as a scout," he suggested. By now he knew he wouldn't convince Silas to turn back, so he tried the next best option. "The person we send can come back with news of the rebels' weaknesses. Then we'd know how to plan an attack."

Rae disagreed with him. "No," she said firmly. "We stay together."

"We die together, you mean," Jesse shot back, wanting to get in the last word. What were the chances they could get inside the headquarters, find Parvel, and escape alive? Jesse wasn't sure, but he knew they couldn't be good.

"The tunnel ends up ahead," Rae said, pointing to a stack of boulders that blocked any further passage. *Maybe there's nothing here after all.* As uneasy as Jesse had been about storming the Rebellion's fortress, even he felt disappointed at the dead end.

"Halt," a harsh voice commanded.

Silas reached to his side to grip his dagger, but found nothing there.

"There," Rae said, pointing to the rock formation in front of them.

Buried deep in the shadows was a wooden door. *There must be some kind of hole for a guard to look out of.* The voice came again. "State your business."

"Three new recruits," Silas said. "From Caven."

"Very good," the voice said, without much enthusiasm. "Sign and password, please."

Silas looked at Jesse and Rae in panic. "You were the one who kept the stone," Jesse said, in a calm voice, hoping desperately that was the sign the sentry spoke of. It was all he could think of, anyway. "Remember? In your pack."

The voice from the door said nothing. *Maybe that means I'm right. The sign is the Rebellion stone. But what is the password?*

"What was the first riddle?" Rae whispered to him as Silas pretended to dig around in his pack. Thankfully, he had realized the need to stall for time even though he held the Rebellion stone in his hand.

"Here in stone are riddles three, symbols of your destiny. Those who solve them soon will find the key for entrance is the mind," Jesse recited automatically. *We already know that the riddles are the password. But which one?*

"Hurry up," the voice demanded.

There was no more time. Silas stepped forward and held the stone up to the slit in the door. "Very good," the voice said, sounding bored. "And the password?"

Again, Silas shot Jesse a desperate look. Jesse's mind whirled frantically, but he could not find the answer.

"The mind," Rae blurted, stepping forward. "The password is the mind."

Silence from behind the door. Then, slowly, it began to creak open.

"That was quick thinking," Jesse muttered to Rae as they walked through the door, trying not to trip over anything in the dark.

She shrugged slightly. "The rhyme said, 'The key for entrance is the mind.' I think literally."

Inside, a torch on the wall provided more light than Jesse's eyes were accustomed to after an hour in the caves. As his eyes adjusted, he looked around. They were inside another tunnel, this one tighter and shorter than the others. A woman with long blonde hair stood in the center of it, wearing a tunic dress, much like the one Rae wore, only gray. If it weren't for the red sash she wore, she would have blended in completely with the rocks around her.

"Follow me," she said, and with a start, Jesse realized it was her voice they had heard through the door. It had been so low and harsh he had assumed it was a man's.

She turned the corner, into a larger cavern, where a row of armed, scarred fighters, men and women, sat on the ground. *The rebels.* There were more than Jesse had expected, at least twenty. A few stood and walked over to the woman.

"Come in," she said, smiling at the three Youth Guard members. Then she pulled out a sword and held it to Jesse's throat. "We've been expecting you."

CHAPTER 10

Jesse hadn't complained when they marched him through the hall of jeering rebels, when they made him sit on the cavern floor with his hands on his head, or when they searched him for weapons.

But when the blonde woman tried to take his walking stick, he grabbed it back. *This is worth fighting for.*

"So, the meek one finally raises his head," the woman said, a smile curling onto her face. "Interesting."

"I need this to walk with," Jesse said stiffly, pointing to his crippled leg. They couldn't take the staff from him. It was all he had to remind him of Kayne—to remind him of home.

The blonde woman frowned, seeming to notice his leg for the first time. Then she leaned over and ripped his right sleeve up. Jesse knew what she was looking for—the tattoo of the Youth Guard, branded into the shoulders of its members. "Why, this one is not of the Guard at all! How amusing." She laughed, and Jesse's face burned with shame.

"I'm glad you're so amused, Sonya," the other woman in the group said. This one had short brown curls and calm, wise eyes. "I, for one, am concerned."

"And why is that, Anise?" one of the men asked.

"Because squads are made of four," she replied, never looking away from Sonya. "We have one already."

A spike of relief went through Jesse's body. *Parvel! He must be alive.* "Here are two others," the woman called Anise continued. "Where is the fourth?"

For a moment, Sonya's cocky smile faded, and Anise pressed on. "Waiting outside with a troop of Patrol, perhaps, ready to attack if they do not return to the surface? Hiding in the tunnels to surprise us as we sleep?"

Now the party of rebels seemed to grow uneasy, muttering to each other. A few more joined the group, staring down at them with a strange mixture of fear and hostility.

"What of it, then?" Sonya demanded. "Where is the fourth?" Jesse looked at Silas and Rae, who were both staring straight ahead. He did the same. *It would be to our advantage,* he realized, *if they believed an attack was coming.*

"Recall," Sonya said casually, "we do have your friend. Despite the insistence of my fellow leaders that we wait for the Nine to assemble, he is, I assure you, quite... disposable."

"She died," Jesse said immediately. "During training. I don't remember her name—what was it, Silas?"

"Aleiah," Silas replied. He did not seem angry with Jesse for answering. *Parvel cannot die for the sake of one who is already dead.* "Sixteen years old, from District Three, near the border of the Northern Waste. It was during an intense training run in the last week before the Festival." He looked dully up at Sonya's suspicious face. "They said they found her only a quarter of a mile from the end."

"Convenient," she snarled at them, "that you would lose a warrior so easily, then replace her with a cripple."

She took back Jesse's staff, this time with her hand on her sword in case he reached for it again.

This time, though, Jesse had greater concerns. "It's true," Jesse insisted. "Ask Parvel if you want a confirmation."

"Send Cotter," Anise said to one of the men. "The prisoner knows him."

The man nodded and ran though an archway into another cavern. "May I have my walking stick back now?" Jesse asked.

"Why?" Sonya asked, eyeing him with suspicion.

"Because," Jesse said, his face perfectly serious, "if I press the phoenix's head, the wood falls away to reveal a sword."

Sonya stared suspiciously at the stick. A few of the other Rebellion members chuckled. Realizing her mistake, she straightened and glared at Jesse. "So he's a cripple *and* a jester."

"What?" Jesse asked in surprise. He looked down at his left leg, as if surprised. "That's right—I *am* crippled. That would explain the walking stick, wouldn't it? I wondered, because the sword feature never seemed to work."

More stifled laughter, especially from a man with a pointy black beard. Jesse made sure to remember his face. *He may be one we could get on our side.*

"You think I will stoop to accommodate one who insults me?" Sonya demanded, her face turning red.

"Oh, let the boy have his staff, Sonya," the man with the black beard said dismissively. "It will do you no harm.

Besides, you saw he's not even of the Guard. What can he do to you?"

"Fine," Sonya replied in disgust, "have it your way, Nathan." She shoved the walking stick toward Jesse.

She snatched up Silas' Rebellion stone instead. "I take it you found this where we kidnapped your friend."

Silas didn't answer. He just stared straight ahead in stony silence.

Sonya glared at all of them now, leaning in and speaking in a low tone. "We sent two men to dispose of you wretches. Only one came back. If I ever find out which one of you killed him, death will be a mercy for you."

None of them said anything, but Jesse had to fight to keep from shivering. The look in Sonya's eyes was pure hatred. If she knew Silas shot the arrow that killed her Rebellion friend…. Jesse didn't want to think about what would happen.

"Here," Sonya said, shoving the stone back into Silas' hands. "Keep it. Let it be a reminder of who the strong and brave in Amarias really are."

For a moment, Jesse was sure Silas was going to shout at Sonya or spit at her feet. But, although his face tightened, he still said nothing.

The man who had run into the cavern came back. "Cotter got the same story out of the other one," he said.

"Good," Sonya said, nodding in satisfaction. "Well, let's get on with it! Tie them up!"

Three of the group stepped forward, tying the three intruders' hands securely behind their backs. Sonya herself checked on Jesse's, giving them a vicious yank before the knot was tied. "You watch what you say to me, boy," she whispered harshly into his ear. "I and the others of the Nine hold all of your lives in balance."

Jesse refused to acknowledge her. *Or cower before her, like she probably wants.*

"All right," ordered Nathan, the black-bearded man. "To the pits."

Jesse couldn't figure out who was in charge in this Rebellion base. First one member would give orders, then another. *Maybe it has something to do with 'the Nine' Sonya is a part of.*

They were practically shoved through the hall by a few men who, Jesse knew, would be ready to pull out their swords should any of them try to escape. *Not that we would be able to do anything with our hands tied.*

The hall led to a tunnel, which led to another, smaller hall. Jesse stopped to look around at it. Along one wall was a stone bench, or perhaps a platform. Before he could see more, the rebel behind him pushed him forward.

"Excuse me," he said to the man marching behind him. "May I ask you a question?"

No one answered. Jesse decided to ask anyway. "What is this 'Nine' that everyone speaks of?"

"The Council of Nine," a voice beside him replied. It was Nathan. "You might call it the ruling structure of the District Two Rebellion. There are, of course, nine of us. Most have already arrived for the spring gathering. The rest will arrive tomorrow."

"The rest?"

"My wife and I are two of the Nine," Nathan replied. "Another is Sonya. You've already met her, of course."

"Pleasant woman that one," Jesse said. *And I suppose it's not good for us that she's in charge here.*

"You gave her little reason to be," Nathan pointed out.

"*I* thought it was amusing. And I didn't say half of what I wanted to say."

Jesse could have been imagining it, but he thought he heard Nathan chuckle. "Nevertheless," he said, clearing his throat and coming to stand beside Jesse, "you and your friends would do well to make no more enemies. In the Council, the majority rules, and you will be facing plenty who wish you dead immediately."

Suddenly, Jesse's jokes didn't seem quite so funny. "And the Nine will meet tomorrow?" he asked, just to be sure.

Nathan nodded. "Which means you may have only one day left to live."

Cheery thought for a cheery place, Jesse decided as they entered the cavern that held the pits.

"Pits" was a fitting name. Unlike a formal prison, the Rebellion's pits were two holes in the stone ground, each covered with a thick metal grate.

The rebels stopped them at the mouth of the first, largest pit. "Hold still," Nathan commanded, jerking Jesse's arms up. Although Jesse could not see, he guessed Nathan was sawing away at the ropes with his sword.

"Careful," Jesse muttered, trying not to move. As the ropes fell away, he felt the welcome sensation of blood flowing back to his hands. "Thank you."

One of the rebels knelt to the ground to unlock the grate. "No sudden moves," Nathan warned all three of them.

What are we going to do, kick him into the pit? What would that accomplish?

The grate slid away and clanked to the ground. One of the men took down a shaky-looking wooden ladder, leaning against the wall, and shoved it into the pit. "All right, in you go."

"How deep is it?" Rae asked.

"About six spans," the man replied.

Spans. Jesse knew that was the unit of measurement in District Two, but he wasn't sure how long it actually was.

Nathan glanced down at the pit. "If the tall one"—by that he meant Silas—"stood at the bottom and raised his arm up, he would be able to reach halfway to the grate," he supplied helpfully.

Jesse peered over the edge. Though the light was very dim—only one of the men in the party carried a torch—he could see nothing but bare rock and shadows at the bottom.

"Not very welcoming," he mused.

"You should have thought of that before you stormed our headquarters," one of their captors shot back.

"I had other things on my mind while making that decision," Jesse informed him, "like saving my friend's life." He assumed Parvel was being kept in the other pit, so he spoke louder than necessary. *Maybe he'll hear me.*

"A lot of good that plan is now," the man said, chuckling.

Jesse felt the irrational urge to whack him with his staff.

Instead, he began climbing down the ladder while Silas held it. It was a slow, painful process, even when he tried to put most of his weight on his good leg. As usual, he felt ashamed for always being the weakest.

The others descended much more quickly. Jesse was just grateful that though it creaked loudly, the ladder held Silas' weight. As soon as Rae, the last one, stepped on the ground, the ladder was pulled up. Then, with a loud clang, the Rebellion members closed the metal grate and locked it. The sound of heavy boots on stone and the fading glow of the torch signaled their retreat, leaving Jesse, Rae, and Silas in almost complete darkness.

The pit was large enough to fit perhaps a dozen prisoners, though Jesse doubted the secret hideout ever saw that many intruders. There seemed to be nothing in the pit but a few rock formations. *Apparently the Rebellion did not see the need to smooth obstacles out of their prison pits.*

"Everyone all right?" Jesse asked.

"Yes," Rae said, next to him.

"Yes," said Silas, a distance away. He was staring up at the grate.

"Yes."

Jesse blinked. *Did Silas repeat himself?*

One of the rock formations moved, and Jesse almost cried out, until it began to speak. "You know, you really did not have to join me here," a familiar voice said courteously. "The company was a bit dull, but, other than that, I was doing quite fine by myself."

Jesse grinned in the dark. "Parvel!"

"Yes, Jesse." He came closer. "And though I wish you were not here with me, I am glad you are alive. I was beginning to wonder."

"Ha," Rae scoffed. "No Da'armon riffraff could get rid of us that easily. You should have known that."

"I was not worried about that, Rae," Parvel replied, a hint of a smile in his voice. "I was more concerned that you and Silas would come to blows."

Jesse laughed at that.

"Not to disturb the reunion," Silas broke in, "but why are we still alive? They know we are Youth Guard."

"True," Parvel said, his voice immediately serious. "I am under the impression that only their Council of Nine can make a decision about us. That is why I have been held here for—well, it must be almost a week now."

"Six days," Jesse corrected.

"But what could they possibly have to decide?" Silas pointed out. "Their goal is to destroy the king. We serve the king."

"Not anymore," Rae said darkly.

That gave Jesse an idea. "She's right. I wonder, if we told the Council the truth about the king—how he's trying to kill the Youth Guard, if…."

"What?" Parvel burst out. "Did I hear you correctly?"

Of course. Parvel hadn't been with them in the desert when Captain Demetri had told Jesse the real purpose of the Youth Guard.

"I'm afraid so," Jesse said. He took a few minutes to explain what he had learned: that creating the Youth Guard was the king's way of finding and eliminating the brightest and strongest young people in the kingdom who might rebel against his reign.

Silence for a moment. Then Parvel cleared his throat. "Well. That ought to make things more interesting."

In a way, Jesse was disappointed. He was hoping for a stronger reaction from Parvel. "You don't sound surprised."

"My father was a member of the king's court," Parvel replied. "I did not know about his designs for the Youth Guard, but no evil report about King Selen surprises me. He is a twisted, corrupt man."

"Do you think if we tell the Rebellion our story they'll let us go?" Jesse asked.

There was a pause as Parvel considered this. "Perhaps," he said at last. "It means we have a common enemy, at least. But many of the Rebellion seem very rash, almost...."

"Bloodthirsty," Silas finished bitterly. "Like they want any excuse to kill, even if it means killing someone innocent."

"I would not put it so strongly," Parvel said, "but, yes, a few come close to that description. Among the Nine, I cannot guess how many would be on our side. I know one who certainly will not be: one called Roland."

"How do you know?" Jesse asked.

"He's a swaggering brute, pompous as a peahen. He came to visit me once. Yesterday, I think it was, although it's hard to keep track of time down here. He insisted it would be of no use to keep me alive, because you would never consider coming back for me."

"Well, here we are," Silas said.

Parvel leaned back against the stone wall. "Tell me, what have you been doing since you left Mir?"

"That's a longer story than I wish to tell," Rae said. "Although I'm sure Jesse would be willing."

"Here in the dungeon, time is one thing we will not lack."

"First, your story," Jesse said. "Tell us how you were taken from Mir."

"Of course," Parvel said. "Hector, one of the Nine, boasted about it our entire journey here. He and another man—Reid was his name—were sent to the crossroads at Mir to find our squad and bring us all here. They planned to ask for a large ransom in exchange for our lives."

"It can't be true," Silas protested. "That man tried to kill you—would have killed all of us."

"Perhaps so," Parvel admitted. "But he was acting on his own, against orders from the Rebellion. Hector said he was quite the radical. He didn't sound terribly sad about Reid's death."

Jesse shuddered a little, remembering back to that night. Silas, a stranger to him then, had appeared at his uncle's inn, saying he had shot the man who had attacked them. Jesse couldn't imagine treating death so casually. *I wonder if I'll ever have to kill anyone to defend my friends.* He didn't like the thought.

"At any rate," Parvel continued, "when Reid didn't return, Hector waited for seven days, as is customary for members of the Rebellion. He would have left town then, but for a bit of conversation he heard from a certain innkeeper who'd had a little too much to drink—a strange story about a sick Youth Guard member who was taken to a shack in the woods."

"Uncle Tristan," Jesse practically groaned. Why would he think his uncle would keep the three Youth Guard members' secret?

"Once he suspected I was still in Mir, Hector simply waited for an opportunity. In my weakened state, I could hardly fight back when he entered my room." Parvel shrugged. "After a few days of forced travel, they threw me in here."

"We never should have left you," Rae said. "None of this would have happened."

"Don't be foolish," Parvel said. "I was the one who told you to leave. In any case, at least one good thing came out of all this. Hector is one of the Nine, and I believe we have a friend in him. We discussed much on our journey here."

"And what happens if, by some miracle, we can persuade them to let us go?" Rae asked. "Where will we go?"

Jesse thought about that and realized with a start that he didn't know. "We escaped from Captain Demetri twice before," he said, "but only barely. We can't go home, or we'll endanger our families. We can't go back to Da'armos, because we're wanted for attempted theft and escaping arrest."

"Then what do we do?" Parvel asked.

Jesse glanced at the others in the darkness. "We were hoping you would be able to answer that."

More silence. "Well," Parvel said, a bit more grimly. "I always say that when ideas don't come, it's probably time for sleep. You must be tired." With that, he laid down on the stone. "Good night."

But it was not a good night, not for Jesse. The stone floor of the pit was cold and uncomfortable, and a thousand questions tumbled through his mind, like a rock slide.

Go to sleep, he commanded himself, closing his eyes. *You'll never get the answers by thinking about them more.*

Sleep wouldn't come. At least, Jesse didn't think it had. With everything so dark, the line between wakefulness and sleep was hard to distinguish.

Beside him, he heard Parvel muttering. "What are you doing?" Jesse asked quietly, so he wouldn't wake Silas and Rae.

"Praying," Parvel said. "Just like I told you I would. I haven't stopped since you left me in Mir."

"Oh. Well, it hasn't done much good."

"What do you mean?" Parvel asked incredulously. "You're here, aren't you?"

"And locked in the same pit as you!"

For a moment, there was silence, and Jesse felt bad for his harsh words. "I just don't understand how you can believe in an invisible God."

"You're right. I can't see God. But I can see what He's done in my life."

Jesse snorted at that. *He sounds exactly like Noa, with all his talk of faith and a 'greater story.'* "Then what is He doing now, Parvel? How could being trapped in this pit be a part of God's plan?"

"Jesse," Parvel said, "if I told you the medallion around my neck has a red dragon with an emerald eye on it, would you believe me?"

Jesse blinked at the abrupt change of subject. "Well, yes. You should know. It's your medallion."

"But I can't see it," Parvel pressed. "How do I know?"

The answer was simple, too simple, but Jesse gave it anyway. "The only reason you can't see it is because it's too dark right now. You've seen it before, when it was light."

"And I'll see it again, once there's light again."

"I suppose," Jesse agreed, still a bit confused.

"It's the same way with faith in God," Parvel said. "I've seen God in the easy times, in the light. And even in the hard times, when I don't see what God is doing, when I don't understand, it doesn't mean I never will—God just hasn't chosen to bring it to light yet. He is still God. And I'm perfectly content to trust Him, even in the dark."

Jesse thought about that for a minute. "I guess I don't have your faith."

"Sometimes a leap into the darkness is the only way to the light," Parvel said. "You're right. It takes faith. But I know God exists, as surely as I know light exists, even though I don't see it right now."

Jesse sighed. He was too tired for that level of deep thinking. "Good night, Parvel," he said.

"Good night. I'll *see* you in the morning."

"Very funny." Jesse tried to get comfortable by shifting positions on the ground. It didn't work. He closed his eyes anyway, hoping to dream about someplace warm and sunny.

The next thing Jesse knew, footsteps were coming toward them. He guessed from the impression of the stones on his face he must have slept, but he didn't feel any less exhausted.

"Ah, we have a visitor," Parvel observed, sitting up from where he was slumped on the ground. Then he raised his voice. "Cotter, is that you?"

"Yes," a voice called in response. The orange glow of a torch came closer, and the round face of a young boy, framed with curly black hair, peered down into the pit.

"The son of two of the Council members," Parvel explained to them. "Thirteen years old. He and I are friends."

Jesse blinked in surprise. He wouldn't have guessed the boy was any older than ten or eleven.

"Breakfast, I assume, Cotter?" Parvel glanced at Jesse. "The food here is terrible, as you might imagine, but it's nice to talk to someone besides our bad-tempered jailers."

He made the comment louder than he needed to, as if he expected the boy to laugh.

But Cotter shook his head. "Not this time, Parvel. The Nine have arrived. Father will be coming soon to bring you up and present you before them."

"Ah," Parvel said, suddenly serious. "And what do you think the verdict will be?"

"I don't know," Cotter said, looking at the torch in his hand instead of at them.

"Cotter," Parvel said sternly. "A boy of your age ought to know to tell the truth, even when it's unpleasant."

The boy bit his lip. "I'm not sure," he said, "but my father and mother are more moderate than most of the Nine, and even they don't know what to do." He took a deep breath. "I don't think it will be good."

CHAPTER 11

Jesse imagined it would be frightening to stand before the group of nine hardened warriors under any circumstances. *But it doesn't help we're awaiting their judgment, with our lives at stake.*

He surveyed the panel of faces staring back at him, none of them smiling. They were seated on the bench he had seen before, carved out of stone. Behind them a row of large torches were lashed to the wall, bright enough to give the entire hall a dim glow. Silas, Rae, Parvel, and Jesse stood in a line in front of them. They were the only others in the cave, according to Council law, they had been told.

Sonya, of course, Jesse recognized, and Anise and Nathan. Parvel had muttered to him that they were Cotter's parents. Hector, the one who had kidnapped Parvel, sat on the far left. But the others were strangers to him—four men and one woman.

I wonder where the other rebels are, Jesse thought briefly. *I assume in the main hall by the entrance. Which is good for us. I doubt a jeering, impatient crowd would side with us.*

Their hands were left untied, probably because all nine of the assembled rebels had weapons. Jesse guessed they were experts at using them—the very best of the Rebellion.

An old man in the center of the group stood. "This meeting of the Council of Nine is now called to order," he announced.

The man at his right side then stood. "First, sentencing of the four Youth Guard members."

"Three Youth Guard and one cripple," Sonya modified, glancing at Jesse smugly. It was all Jesse could do to ignore the comment.

"I say we have no choice," she continued, leaping to her feet. As he saw her standing tall and proud before them, Jesse realized Sonya was actually quite beautiful. *To anyone who doesn't know her, that is.*

"They have found our headquarters," Sonya said. "If we release them, they will report to the king. Our meeting place—the only one that has never been discovered—would be destroyed, and we would be scattered. They must die."

Several of the Nine turned to discuss this with each other, and Jesse realized that a Council member only stood when he or she wanted to address the entire group. Apparently, the Nine were allowed to talk to each other freely throughout the meeting. *This might take longer than we expected. Which, since Cotter expects the outcome to be bad, doesn't bother me.*

Now a man with a thick, matted gray beard stood, and the rest fell silent. Although he had sharp features and a direct, pointed stare, Jesse didn't sense the same hostility from him that he did whenever Sonya spoke. "If it pleases the Nine, I would like to hear an account of how these three managed to find their way here at all."

"I say we quit wasting our time and declare them guilty," a large, burly man countered, standing. "We can see they serve the king—whatever lies they tell won't change that."

"Roland," Parvel muttered. Jesse wasn't surprised. His face seemed locked in a scowl, and he directed it right at them.

"It may, or it may not," the gray-bearded man said. "But, regardless, would it not be wise to consider how to prevent future intruders from reaching our headquarters?"

Most of the Nine nodded, except Roland, who sat down with his arms crossed. "Well," Nathan said to them, not bothering to stand. "You heard Mathias. Let's hear your story."

Silas and Rae both looked to Jesse, and he began to breathe heavier. Of course, his people were storytellers. But this was no simple tale told at a glowing fireplace hearth on a cold night. It was an account given in front of a group of people who wanted to kill him.

"Include as much detail as possible," Parvel whispered. "The more they know about us, the less likely they are to see us merely as faceless intruders. It will make it harder for them to vote against us."

"Well?" Sonya again, her lips curling into a sneer. "Are you mute as well as lame?"

Jesse took a deep breath and stepped forward. "Our story begins when we realized Parvel was taken from my friend's house in Mir."

Each detail of the story began to fall into place: Kayne describing what had happened to Parvel, Bern and New Urad, Noa and his histories, the pile of rocks, and especially the Patrol members who pursued them and created the cave-in to kill them. Jesse decided it was an important detail, since the Rebellion hated the king and his men.

Jesse tried to make his story as dramatic as possible, and judging by the interested faces of the Nine, he succeeded. Only Sonya and Roland, sneering and staring into the distance with a bored expression, seemed not to be listening. He pressed on without giving them time to interrupt with an objection or complaint. Whenever he needed encouragement, he just glanced over at Parvel, who was listening intently, delighted at every twist and turn in the plot.

Then Jesse spoke of the riddles and how they solved them: the near fall into the ravine, the choice between the diamond and moon tunnels, and how Rae discovered the password. "And so," Jesse concluded, "that was how we found the headquarters in Riddler's Pass."

"Riddler's Pass?" the gray-bearded man, Mathias, questioned.

"That is what the Roarics call this place," Jesse explained. "It seemed a fitting name."

The oldest member of the Nine, the one who sat in the center, smiled at that and Jesse briefly wondered why.

"You see?" Mathias said, standing. "You have heard these young people are no friends of the king. They are intelligent and clever, and no doubt understand what we are trying to do here. They will not betray us. I am confident of this."

Now three stood at once—Sonya, Roland, and Anise. Instead of talking at once, Sonya and Roland nodded at Anise. *Strange.* Then Jesse realized, *It must be that the eldest is allowed to speak first.* Anise seemed to be a few years older than Sonya or Roland, who appeared to be the youngest of the Nine.

"But they *are* Guard," Anise pointed out. "How can we be sure their true loyalties do not lie with the king?"

Sonya and Roland sat after she did. *Clearly, they were going to say the same thing.*

"With all due respect," Jesse said, a hint of a smile edging onto his face, "the king is trying to kill us. That hardly gives us much reason to support him."

A few of the Nine nodded, and one even chuckled a little. "It's true," Jesse heard someone whisper.

"Then why did the traitors join the Guard?" Roland burst out, forgetting to stand. "Tell us that."

"We didn't know," Jesse said, but even he knew the answer sounded hollow.

"I'll tell you why I joined the Guard," Rae said, stepping forward. Her dark eyes were blazing with an intensity Jesse had never seen before. "I joined because my village was starving. The king took away all of our food every harvest, leaving us with barely enough to survive."

Suddenly, Jesse felt a new sympathy for Rae. *Why didn't she ever tell us?*

"My village chose me to represent them at the muster. People I did not even know helped me train, even gave me extra rations of their food, so I could join the Guard, complete my mission, and use the spectacular reward promised to save my family and friends." Rae's voice became flat. "I was their last hope."

There were a few mutters of approval and sympathy, and Jesse knew Rae's passionate words had struck home.

"But how do we know?" Sonya asked. "Perhaps all of this is just a ruse to gain our trust. As soon as they are let go, they will report us to the Patrol and collect a reward."

On and on it went, with Mathias and Hector arguing in their favor, Sonya and Roland firmly against them, each standing and repeating the same arguments. There was talk of torture, of pardons, of issues and accusations that seemed completely unrelated to the case at hand.

Finally, the white-haired man who had called the meeting to order and had not spoken since stood and cleared his throat. "It is pointless to continue this argument. We must not stand here, indecisive, like the stones around us."

"Then call the vote!" Roland declared. "Death or release!"

The old man gave him a pointed stare and continued. "Perhaps there is a third option," he said, his words clear and measured. "We let them live—if they agree to join us."

Now Sonya stood. "I object, sir. How can we trust them?"

"We keep one here at all times," the old man replied. Clearly, he had put much thought into this. "Can we doubt they have great loyalty to each other? The three risked their lives to save the first by coming here at all. As long as we have the power of life or death over one, they will not waver in their commitment."

Silas' face was as hard as stone, but his eyes were boiling with anger. Jesse glanced at Parvel in panic. *This is not what we want!*

Parvel just shook his head slightly, turning back to listen to the old man.

Hector stood. "I agree with Gregor," he said. "These four—or three, if we keep one in the pits—will do more for our cause than dozens of our best fighters. The king keeps them in his service for a reason. They could be a powerful force against him."

There was a murmuring in the hall as the Council discussed the idea. "No," Silas hissed to Parvel, his fists knotted at his sides. "I will never join them. Not even to save our lives."

"Calm yourself, Silas," Parvel said. "And for goodness' sake, let me talk to them. You'll only anger them more."

Silas didn't seem to like this piece of advice, but he pressed his mouth into a hard, firm line.

Now Nathan stood. "We'll consider the option," he said. "I, for one, see the reason in it." He looked directly at each of the four in turn. "But I wonder what these four think about joining our cause."

Parvel stepped forward immediately. *Probably so Silas wouldn't have a chance.* "I appreciate your generous offer—I realize that only a dedicated, worthy few are asked to join the Rebellion. But, as I have already explained to Hector, there are many points where I disagree sharply with the Rebellion."

"See!" Sonya declared triumphantly. "He is on the side of the king."

"What is all this talk of sides?" he demanded, his fists tightening. He began to pace in front of the Nine. "From you, from others. With the king or with the Rebellion? Has the time passed when a man—or even a young person, as you call us—can do what is right, without taking a side?"

"Don't let his fancy words deceive you," Roland interrupted. "They're nothing but lies. He'll turn on us in a second."

"That is your ego speaking, not your mind," Anise said calmly, again without a trace of anger. "His words reflect what I myself have considered more than once. I wish to hear more." She nodded at Parvel. "Continue."

"Do I believe the king is wrong? Of course," Parvel said. "But I also believe the Rebellion is wrong." The faces of the Nine hardened.

Nathan stood again. "And why is that?"

Before Parvel could reply, Hector stood. "The boy has many opinions," he said smoothly. Though his words were to Nathan, he stared straight at Parvel. *He is warning him not to continue.* "That doesn't change the fact that he is harmless to us."

Nathan did not sit on the rock bench. "Thank you, Hector, but I asked him the question."

Parvel nodded. "Why is the Rebellion wrong? Because you cannot fight evil with more evil," he said, emphasizing his words strongly. "You who accuse the king of stealing your food resort to stealing if it advances your cause. You who claim your freedom is restricted by the curfew take away the freedom of others. You who deplore the killing of innocents will kill innocents yourselves."

At that last point, Roland stood again. "It's the price we have to pay for freedom," he growled. "There are costs to any great effort."

Beside him, Jesse could hear Silas' heavy breathing. *Stay silent*, he willed him. *It won't do any good for you to speak now.*

"Let me ask you this," Parvel said, stepping forward again. "Let's say I was locked in the king's dungeon at Terenid. After stealing the key away from the guard, I made a dramatic escape. In the process, one of the guards shot at me with his crossbow. I grabbed the nearest servant boy and used him as a shield. The arrow struck him, and he died. Would that be wrong?"

"No," Nathan said, sounding defensive. "You had to save your own life. You were trying to escape. The boy just happened to be in the wrong place at the wrong time."

"I see," Parvel said, looking thoughtful. "Now, let's change the scene. Imagine that I am locked in a pit within Riddler's Pass."

Jesse snorted. *Yes, that takes a great deal of imagination.*

"After ripping off my ropes with brute strength, I made a dramatic escape," Parvel continued. "In the process, I was chased by a number of the Rebellion. In my panic, I shoved the nearest pursuer, a young boy named Cotter, into a deep ravine, killing him."

Anise gasped, and rage filled Nathan's face. "Would that be wrong?" Parvel asked coolly.

"Of course!" Anise exclaimed, glaring at him. It was the first time Jesse had seen her show any emotion. "Of course it would be!"

"And yet," Parvel said, in that same thoughtful tone, "the same argument applies. I had to save my own life. I was trying to escape. The boy just happened to be in the wrong place at the wrong time."

None of the Nine said a word. "Never fear, Anise," Parvel said, looking straight at her. "I agree with you—it would not be right. But your reaction proves my point: there are certain things we know should never be done."

Then, louder, he declared to the entire hall, "Either all killing of innocents, when necessary, is acceptable, or it is not acceptable under any circumstances. There is no middle ground. Not in matters of life and death."

"Enough," Sonya declared, leaping to her feet. "*We* are not on trial here. Give us your answer—will you join us or not?"

Jesse could see where this was leading, and he did not like it. As soon as they answered no, they would be killed. *But we cannot say yes.* Parvel's words had made that clear.

But here in the hall, there is no chance of escape. Although no other rebels were present, the Nine were all heavily armed. Even if the others could run back to the tunnels that led to the surface, Jesse, with his lame leg, would be caught almost immediately.

Here we have no hope. But if we can get away, even for a few minutes....

Jesse stepped forward. "I, for one, don't agree with Parvel." Jesse could see Parvel turn to him in surprise. Jesse willed him to understand, or at least hold off his judgment until he could explain. "We have to save our own lives, just as you have to protect your families and fight for justice. I will join the Rebellion."

"I'm with Jesse," Rae said.

Jesse tried not to show the surprise he felt. *She's not pretending.*

"I am tired of sitting and doing nothing while the king ruins our lives," she said heatedly. "It's time to act."

"Action alone is not right," Parvel argued. "It must be the right kind of action."

"And I'm not sure the Rebellion's kind is not right," Jesse threw in.

"Jesse, Rae, both of you are wrong," Parvel said. "You have to let go of your hate. It cannot solve anything."

Rae just shook her head. "You don't understand. The king and the Rebellion mean nothing to you, because you haven't been wronged by them. You don't know what it's like to experience injustice."

Parvel looked right at Rae. "You are wrong about that," he said quietly. "The Youth Guard took my brother five years ago. And that turned my father into a distant, angry man."

His brother was in the Youth Guard? Jesse had not known.

"You see?" Rae said. "The king killed Parvel's brother, like he's trying to kill us. We have to join the Rebellion."

Silas turned to her, his gray eyes flaming with rage, like the glowing rocks of the Deep Mines. "How can you say that knowing what you know?"

Rae took a step backward, hesitation in her eyes. Then she shook her head. "No, Silas. This is our only chance."

"They killed my father," Silas shouted, and the accusation echoed in the cave. Now some of the Nine began to murmur.

"And the king is killing my family, my entire village," Rae countered, her quieter voice holding every bit as much fire as Silas' roar.

A perfect, even split. Jesse could not have asked for anything better if he had planned it in advance.

"There is a better way," Parvel insisted.

"That is what I have been told all my life, and I won't listen anymore," Rae said.

"Are you blind? Joining them will destroy us!" Silas shouted.

"You don't understand!" Parvel answered.

Their voices rose to shouts, and Jesse gave up trying to listen, or even argue intelligently.

"I say you are willing to squander our lives for your futile ideals."

"…don't understand what you're doing…."

"Tell the starving, the dying of my village about your better way. I will not…."

"…might be the only way to save our lives, and…."

"…become a traitor to all you swore to defend."

"What about justice?"

"What about it? Is the king just?"

"…only care about yourself…."

"Quiet!" Jesse shouted. His outburst shocked them enough to listen, and he turned to the Nine. "We must all give the same answer," he said. "I think we all agree on that. But we should not disturb the Council with our discussion. If you will provide an escort back to the pits, we'll decide among ourselves and leave you to discuss our fate among yourselves."

"Wise advice," Gregor, the old man in the center, said. He looked around at his fellow Council members. "The others of the Rebellion are not permitted to enter the hall while the Council is meeting. Which of you will take them away?"

No one volunteered. Finally, Roland stood and Jesse again noticed his hulking frame and the large, rough sword at his side. "I will go," he said, walking to the four. "And believe me," he said in a low voice, "if you give me any excuse to run you through, I'll gladly take it."

CHAPTER 13

All the way back to the pits, Roland grumbled about the king, the Youth Guard, the blabbermouths in the Council who forgot they were warriors and not lawyers, and anything else he could think of.

Instead of listening, Jesse tried frantically to think of a plan. *If he puts us back in the pit, we'll be just where we started.* There was no chance of overpowering Roland. They were unarmed, weak, and tired. Besides, Roland kept his hand on his sword at all times, ready to whip it out at the slightest challenge.

Jesse only saw Roland show one weakness, one small act of overconfidence: when they reached the pits he turned away from them to put his torch in one of the holders along the cave wall. It only took a second, but the fact that Roland was foolish enough to turn his back on his enemy gave Jesse a little hope.

He stared at the gaping mouth of the pit. Six spans down, Nathan had said. *Maybe, just maybe....*

Roland took the ladder and shoved it into the pit. "You two first," he said, pointing to Parvel and Silas.

"Not at the same time, I hope," Parvel said. "That ladder ought to be used for firewood. It won't support the weight of two of us."

"You'll go down together if I tell you to," Roland said, glaring at him.

"And I suppose you'll explain our bruises to the Council after the ladder breaks and we fall."

"Who's the one giving orders here? Maybe the king is right to kill off you Youth Guard brats...."

Jesse was glad for the distraction. While Roland and Parvel argued, he leaned over to Rae and whispered a few words of his plan in her ear. A slight nod was the only recognition he got in response.

When Parvel and Silas were down in the pit, Roland nodded at Jesse. "Now you."

Jesse almost laughed. *Apparently he thinks even a cripple is more dangerous than a girl.* He would soon learn otherwise.

"I can't reach the first rung," Jesse said, backing away from the edge of the pit.

Silas and Parvel knew he had been able to climb down the first time. They would know something was coming. Jesse was counting on it.

"It's too far. With my crippled leg and all." Jesse hoped he sounded whiny enough, and that Roland wouldn't decide to heave him into the pit.

Instead, just like Jesse had hoped he would, Roland turned away from him and stooped over the pit. Rae was already edging forward. "Stupid cripple. You're...."

He never got to finish his sentence, because Jesse and Rae

shoved him into the pit. With a startled shout, he toppled into the darkness.

Now Jesse heard other voices—Silas' and Parvel's—mixed with the sounds of struggle. Jesse knelt down by the edge, but he could see nothing but darkness.

One last shout. Then silence. Jesse could hardly breathe.

"Well," Parvel's voice said from the pit, "I don't think they'll let us join the Rebellion now."

Jesse wanted to jump up and down, something he hadn't been able to do since the accident. "Hurry," he said. "Someone might have heard the shouts."

Silas was the first to emerge from the pit. He wiped at a thin cut on his cheek, smearing blood across the back of his hand. "That was dangerous, Jesse. What if Parvel hadn't gotten Roland's sword away from him before he could use it?"

"It was the only thing I could think of," Jesse protested. "Would you rather join the Rebellion or die here?" Silas didn't argue with that.

Parvel came out next, setting Roland's sword on the stone before crawling out of the pit. "Poor fellow is going to have a nasty headache when he wakes up," he said cheerfully. "And a black eye. Maybe two."

In spite of himself, Jesse felt a rush of relief. "So you didn't kill him."

Silas laughed, but it was a hard, harsh laugh. "Look who got the sword, Jesse. If it had been me instead of Parvel, we wouldn't have to worry about Roland anymore." Before Parvel could reach for it, Silas picked up the sword and held it stiffly at his side.

"That's all then," Parvel said, pulling up the ladder and setting it carefully against the wall in its proper place. Silas slammed the heavy gate over the pit and locked it.

"Shh!" Jesse hissed. "Do you want to bring the whole Council running?"

"They might be doing that already," Rae snapped, "which is why we need to get out of here!" She turned and dashed toward the archway in the back of the cavern.

Silas joined her at once, and Parvel took the torch from its holder and followed. As far as Jesse could see, there was only one other way out of the cave besides the entrance that led to the assembly hall of the Nine.

"But we don't know where we're going," Jesse protested, limping as quickly as he could to catch up.

Rae slowed down but didn't stop. "So tell Silas to get out his little map. But I'm not staying around for conversation when dozens of angry rebels could come after us at any second."

They followed her past the archway and into another set of tunnels. Silas pulled the Rebellion stone from his pocket, adding its light to the glow of the torch.

These tunnels seemed to contain caves used as storerooms. Jesse paused for a second in front of one of them and saw food and weapons stacked on wooden shelves on the wall. *They could last weeks in some kind of a siege*, Jesse realized.

Silas fell back to walk beside Jesse. "So your speech to the Rebellion, about wanting to join them," Silas said. "That was just a ploy to get them to send us back here?"

"I was stalling for time," Jesse admitted. He was already

starting to breathe harder. "I didn't have much of a plan. I just knew we had to get out of there."

"So you didn't mean anything you said?" Silas pressed.

"No." Jesse didn't bother to explain that Rae was serious the whole time. That conversation would have to wait for later. Now they needed to find a way out of Riddler's Pass.

They reached a split in the tunnel and stopped. Silas set Roland's sword on the ground and pulled out Noa's map from inside his shirt. He held the map close to the stone, trying to read Noa's small print. "It's a long way to the exit," he said. "Many of the tunnels are unmarked on the map."

That was not good news, especially for Jesse. "I can't run much farther," he said, his face turning red as he admitted it. For a minute, no one said anything.

Silas was the first to speak up. "You go ahead," he said to Rae and Parvel. "I'll stay with Jesse."

"But…" Parvel protested.

"There's no time to argue," Silas said impatiently. "I have a light and the sword." He handed the paper to Parvel. "You can have the map. I memorized the route."

"Are you sure?" Parvel asked, staring at Silas.

"I know every detail of it," Silas said, never looking away. "I knew I would have to, in case it was lost or confiscated. You and Rae find the exit and leave this place. Jesse and I will hide until they go past, then join you once they are gone."

Jesse felt like he should protest and say he would stay alone. But he couldn't bring himself to do it. *I'm afraid,* he admitted to himself, hating the thought, but knowing it was true. *I don't want to be here, in the dark, alone.*

"All right," Parvel said, after a second of hesitation. He glanced at Rae, who looked ready to bolt. "I do not like it, but we appear to have little choice."

"You should take the torch," Rae suggested. "It will provide more light."

Silas looked at her like she was crazy. "And how would we hide the glow when the Rebellion passed by?" He shook his head and clenched the stone tighter. "No. This is all the light we need." He turned to Jesse. "Come on. We must find some place to hide."

Jesse started to follow, but he felt a firm hand on his shoulder holding him back. It was Parvel, and even in the dim light, Jesse could see a worried frown on his face. "Jesse…be careful."

"Silas will be with me," Jesse said, backing toward the tunnel Silas had turned down.

"I know." A pause, then Parvel said quietly, "That's why I'm worried."

Jesse didn't have time to wonder what Parvel meant, because Silas was already too far ahead. His lame leg punished him for the quick steps it took to catch up. *I can't lose him in here, or I'll never find him again.*

At first, they passed caves the rebels clearly used, ones with crates of supplies or blanket rolls for sleeping, as well as glowing stones mounted every few feet to give the caverns a dim glow. But, once they left the main tunnel, the maze that was the Deep Mines took over. *Nothing here but rocks and…more rocks.*

"Why aren't we hiding in one of the storerooms?" Jesse asked. "We could empty a barrel or find a root cellar, or…."

"It's the first place they'd look," Silas interrupted. "We have a better chance in the small tunnels. Look for a small, dark crevice, something easily overlooked and out of the way of the main path."

That didn't sound like a place Jesse would want to hide, but he knew Silas was right. With every step he took, Jesse strained to listen for voices following them. A few times, he thought he heard some, but he wasn't sure if it was real or merely his imagination inventing pursuers.

Once, the path began to narrow. "Careful," Silas warned, pointing to the side with the Rebellion stone. A sudden drop-off was revealed as the glowing stone jutted into the darkness.

Jesse stopped to peer into the canyon. He could see no bottom. *I suppose we won't be hiding there.*

He took a few steps away from the edge and bumped into Silas, who had stopped in front of a small cavern cut into the rock. He had to duck to fit inside. "Here," he called, waving Jesse over.

Jesse limped to the cavern and peered inside. "It's a dead end," he said, seeing the back of the cave even in the dim glow of Silas' Rebellion stone.

"Exactly," Silas said. "If the rebels know the layout of these tunnels—and they must—they will assume we would never run into a cave that leads nowhere. They will search the tunnels leading to the surface."

The logic was good, Jesse knew, but he still didn't like being trapped. "Come on," Silas said, stepping in further. "Behind that boulder. We can both fit."

The boulder was actually a rock formation that seemed to grow like a bulky plant in the very corner of the cave. Jesse went in first, sliding into the narrow space between the formation and the back of the cavern. Silas shoved the Rebellion stone into his pocket and followed, grunting as he tried to wedge his larger frame into the gap.

Jesse tried to calm his breathing, still a bit winded from running. Soon, his heart returned to its normal rate. Still, it sounded like the pounding of a drum in the silence. Jesse hoped no Rebellion members would come near the cave, because if they did, he was sure they would be able to hear the beating of his heart.

Keeping track of time in the dark was impossible. Every time Jesse tried to count the passing seconds, he was distracted by his worries or an imagined sound. Just when he was sure it had been hours and the Rebellion searchers must have given up long ago, he heard voices shouting.

Beside him, Silas stiffened, and Jesse knew that this time, it was not his imagination. The shouting grew louder with every beat of Jesse's heart. They were not close enough for him to discern what they were saying. *But one of them sounds like Roland.*

To take his mind off of the rebels searching for them, Jesse counted his breaths, trying to keep them slow and even. *If they discover us, it will be my fault,* he knew. *Silas could have gotten away if he hadn't waited for me.*

That thought did nothing to calm Jesse. *Stop. You'll only make yourself nervous.* He leaned his head against the rock in front of him. *We'll be fine.*

Though the distant voices got slightly louder, Jesse heard many footsteps run past the tunnel leading to their hiding place. *Going, like Silas said all along, to deeper parts of the cave, where there are more tunnels.*

Another set of footsteps, slower than the others. Jesse caught his breath. *Someone's coming!* If he was hearing correctly, the steps were not distant, like the others. They came from the tunnel.

A dim light eased into Jesse's vision, and he looked down. Silas had taken the Rebellion stone out of his pocket again. He was clutching the stone in one hand, and the white glow surrounding it gave Jesse enough light to see the sword he clutched in the other. His breathing was heavy and his eyes fixed straight ahead.

He wouldn't.... Another glance told Jesse the truth. *He would.* "No," Jesse whispered. "Silas, don't. You'll give us away."

"Let them come," Silas hissed back. "This time, I am ready."

Parvel knew. He had known all along. The footsteps were closer now.

"No," Jesse repeated, desperately trying to break through the steel curtain that seemed to have fallen over Silas' eyes. "Silas, it's wrong."

"So was what they did to my father!"

The anguished whisper was louder than those before it, and the footsteps stopped for a moment. *Maybe he'll go away,* Jesse thought unreasonably.

But the footsteps began again, this time slightly slower, more cautious. Jesse could see the faint glow of a torch. *He'll be ready too*, Jesse realized, his mind trying to think of what to do. *But we can't stay hidden anymore. He knows we're here.*

Their seeker was almost there, the footsteps unbearably loud. With the element of surprise on his side, Silas could easily succeed in his attack, Jesse knew. *Especially with the strength fueled by anger.* They would not be taken away to be executed. They would be able to escape the cavern, able to go safely home to Mir.

But Parvel's words echoed in Jesse's mind. *There is no middle ground. Not in matters of life and death.*

The first flame of the torch came into view in the cave's entrance. With a cry of rage, Silas sprang from behind the boulder, sword raised into the air.

And, even though it went against nearly every instinct he had, Jesse jumped out too. He lunged at Silas, trying to pull his arm down. With a nearly inhuman growl, Silas threw Jesse to the ground in front of him.

Jesse protected his head with his hands as he hit the ground. Slowly, he looked up to see the intruder, almost afraid of what he would find.

There, standing frozen in the entrance of the cave, was Cotter.

Jesse glanced back at Silas, who also hadn't moved. His face was contorted in anger and confusion, his sword still held high. For a moment, neither one appeared to blink or even breathe.

Silas looked down at Jesse for a brief second, and Jesse saw something new in Silas' face. Shame.

Then Silas ran past Cotter into the darkness.

Cotter, blue eyes round with fear, turned to watch him go, but his feet were still frozen to the ground.

Now Jesse was alone. *And I certainly can't run after Silas.* His only hope was Cotter now. *If he calls for the rest of his group, I will be killed.*

"Cotter," Jesse began, trying to think. He stood up slowly, painfully. *Parvel would know what to say.* "I'm not going to hurt you."

Cotter said nothing, but he also did not reach for the oversized sword in the sheath by his side. The sword looked ridiculous on a person so small. *I wonder if he even knows how to use it.*

"All I want to do is leave here," Jesse said, trying to keep his voice even. "I won't betray this place to the Patrol. I just want to go home to my mother and father."

It was the wrong thing to say. Cotter blinked. "Father," he repeated, staring into the dark. Then, backing away from the entrance of the cave, he called, "Here! Someone help! I found one of them!"

I'm trapped. That was the only thought passing through Jesse's mind. He took a limping step toward the entrance. *If I can just get out of this cave....* It wouldn't make any difference in the end, but Jesse felt as if the walls of the small cavern were about to close in on him.

Cotter backed away, and Jesse almost laughed at the ridiculousness of the situation. *He's the one with the sword, not me.* "Careful," he warned, as Cotter took another step out of the cave. "You might...."

Fall. Hmm. That's an idea.

The deep ravine by the path was only a few steps away. Jesse fought to get his thoughts in order and bend them into some kind of plan.

Too late. As soon as he stepped out of the cave, he saw two figures with torches approaching. *Roland and Anise.*

So there it was. Jesse had done it. He had taken Parvel's step of faith into the darkness, tried to take a stand for what was right, and where had it gotten him? Parvel and Rae were probably captured already, Silas had run away, and he was about to face the Rebellion by himself.

God, if You're out there, what did I do wrong? Parvel and Noa said You are in control of everything, so where have You been when I needed You? Where are You now?

No answer.

Jesse backed against the stone wall. It was over. He had never felt so alone.

CHAPTER 14

Roland's laugh echoed in the cave. "Well," he sneered, swaggering toward Jesse. Even Cotter backed away from him a little. "We send the boy down a dead-end tunnel to keep him busy, and he actually finds one of the brats."

He'll kill me right here, Jesse realized. He tensed himself for his next action. *Anise won't be able to stop him.*

That gave him the courage to reach out and grab Cotter's sword from its sheath.

It was not difficult to do. Cotter, who foolishly held his torch in his right hand, could not reach down in time to stop him. By the time Cotter realized what was happening, Jesse held the sword high.

"Don't move," Jesse commanded, seeing Roland edge forward. He grabbed Cotter's arm and yanked him closer. Cotter's face was frozen with fear. "Or I run the boy through."

Anise gasped. Roland stopped moving forward, but his cocky sneer never wavered.

"You two will back into the cave and let me pass," Jesse said, hoping his bold words sounded convincing. "I will take the boy with me until we reach the surface, to ensure we get there safely. If you harm me or any of my friends, or if you try to do anything to stop us, he dies."

"We will go," Anise said immediately, stepping back. She glanced at Roland, who had not moved.

"I don't believe you," Roland said, looking at Jesse.

Jesse wouldn't let a trace of the growing fear he felt show on his face. "Step away," Jesse repeated. He held the sword up to Cotter's throat, the way Sonya had to him when they had first entered the headquarters.

Anise began to sob, pulling at Roland's arm. "Back away, I tell you," she cried, and the desperation in her voice made Jesse sick. "That is my son!"

Roland shook her off with a rough jerk of his arm, and Anise fell to the ground. He stared at Jesse from two bruised, swollen eyes. Even his nose seemed to be bent to one side. *From falling into the pit, no doubt.* Of course, a warrior like Roland wouldn't stay back to have his wounds tended while the four children who tricked him needed to be found.

"You won't take a life to save your own," Roland said. "Your friend said as much to the Nine." He stepped closer, and Jesse edged back, yanking a trembling Cotter with him. *He's trying to drive me over the edge of the ravine.*

Maybe I don't have to kill him, he thought. *I just have to make him bleed a little. Anise will see and pull her own sword on Roland to make him move.*

And what would Parvel's God think of that? Jesse wasn't sure where the thought came from, but he froze, knowing the answer instantly.

"You cannot fight evil with evil," Roland taunted.

And, though Parvel's words were being distorted by the hulking, brutal man, Jesse could not deny their truth.

He let go of Cotter and pushed him away from the edge of the ravine, keeping the sword. *I might yet need it.* "You're right," he said heavily.

Cotter ran to his mother's side, looking back at Jesse in confusion.

"Well, then," Roland said, a cruel smile twisting his face. "I think the Nine would approve of your death now that you've attempted to escape and threatened the life of one of our own. And I consider it a pleasure to carry out the sentence myself."

In one swift move, he drew his sword and struck forward at Jesse. Jesse blocked with his own sword, then darted to the side, trying to get around Roland. *I have to get away from the edge. If I fall, I die.*

But Roland, roaring like a mad bull, got there first. *For a man so large, he can move quickly.* It was easy to see why Roland had become powerful among the Rebellion at such a young age.

His eyes flashing with rage, Roland swung for Jesse's head, and Jesse ducked just in time. With his lame leg, he could not move quickly or take advantage of his smaller size to avoid the blows.

He raised his sword to block another thrust, but this time, Roland twisted his blade around Jesse's. *No!* With a sickening clank of steel, Jesse's sword fell to the ground, and he watched in horror as Roland's boot stomped down and kicked it away.

Laughing loudly, Roland took a step forward, sword raised high, and Jesse stepped back. He glanced quickly over his shoulder. *Only a pace or two before the ravine. I can't go any farther.*

Roland seemed to know this too, because instead of striking Jesse with his sword, he took another small step forward.

This time, Jesse did not move. All he had now was his staff, and he held it out in front of him, hands spread apart, like a shield.

"Oh," Roland sneered. "At least the cripple still has his stick."

Another step. Still, Jesse did not move. *Death by sword, though painful, is better than a slow death, broken and in agony, at the bottom of a cliff.* He wondered at the clearness of his thoughts even right before death.

"You think you're brave, don't you?"

Jesse almost laughed. *Hardly.* But his dry mouth wouldn't let him speak.

"Well," Roland said, shrugging casually, but with evil in his eyes, "if you won't jump, we'll do this my way."

Before Roland could raise his arm back to strike, Jesse swung his staff upright and brought it down on Roland's arm with all his strength. The cracking blow mingled with Roland's gasp of pain, and the sword fell, clanking against the stone. Jesse shot his foot out and kicked it off the edge and into the ravine.

Roland clutched his bruised arm and glared at Jesse. "Why, you…." He roared a wordless shout of anger. "I will finish you myself, with my bare hands."

In that momentary pause, before Roland charged, Jesse heard what he would later describe as a voice inside his mind. Not one that you could actually hear. Almost like a thought.

Stop fighting. Trust me.

But....

It came again. *Stop fighting. Trust me.*

So Jesse stood there, watching as Roland backed up, his fists curled into angry balls. Then, just as Roland, his face twisted with rage, was about to rush forward, he collapsed.

Jesse stared at his fallen form. *What madness is this?*

Then he looked up to see Anise, face stained with tears, holding a large rock high. She dropped it to the ground with a thud, looking stunned. There was a smear of blood on it.

Jesse looked at Roland's fallen form and saw a gash on the back of his head. "Why...why did...?" he stammered.

"Mother!" Cotter exclaimed, staring at Roland with wide eyes.

She stepped back, putting her arm around her son. "Your friend was right," she said to Jesse, quietly. "Perhaps what we do in the Rebellion is wrong. I do not know. But I know this would have been wrong."

Jesse did not know quite what to say. His tired, racing mind was still trying to understand what had happened. He walked away from the ledge and stooped down to pick up Cotter's sword.

"Go," Anise said, pointing to the darkness of the other tunnels. "You don't belong here."

147

Jesse ran a few limping steps, then stopped. "But I don't know the way."

Anise looked uncertain for a moment. "Of course not." She took a deep breath, then set her face in determination. "Come with me."

"Wait. What will happen to you," Jesse asked, hesitating, "for helping me?"

"I may lose my place in the Nine," Anise said, "but then, I may not. Your friend's words had a profound effect on many in the Council." She shook her head. "But come, we must hurry."

"What if he wakes up?" Jesse asked, pointing to Roland. It was easy to see the man was still breathing.

"That," Anise said, "is why we must hurry." She turned to Cotter. "Give me your torch. You must stay behind."

"But…." Cotter protested.

"No," Anise said, interrupting him. "Only the Nine are permitted to know the location of the East Escape."

Cotter nodded and handed his mother his torch. She began to hurry down the path, and Jesse limped behind her, leaving Cotter and Roland in the tunnel. *I hope Cotter leaves too, before Roland wakes.* Jesse didn't want to think about how mean Roland would be after getting hit in the head twice in one day.

It only took Jesse a few minutes of following Anise through the passageways to become completely lost. After a while, he stopped trying to memorize the twists and turns. He just tried to keep up and watch where he stepped—the passageways seemed to be filled with ravines and pits.

Anise, however, seemed to know exactly where she was going. "There is only one way to the surface, other than the riddle tunnels," she explained, as they squeezed through a small cleft in the rock. "That is how we enter and exit the cave, always. This last exit is intended only for emergencies, in case we have to flee from some kind of attack. Only the Nine know its location."

That was not good news to Jesse. *What about Rae, Silas, and Parvel?* Jesse pictured them tied up, in the custody of the rebels. *Or dead, if Sonya was the one who found them.*

"The first archway," Anise pointed to a gap at the end of the tunnel. She tapped a stone near the top as she passed.

There was a moon carved into the stone.

Could we be all the way back at the front of the headquarters again? Then Jesse shook his head. *No. That moon stone was near the ground.*

That left only one other option. *The way out is a reversed copy of the way in.*

Here, the path seemed to be smaller, the rock formations more frequent. *Like hardly anyone uses this place.* Once, walking around the edge of a hole in the path, he thought he saw something move.

"Anise," he said quietly.

She stopped, instantly alert. "What?"

But when Jesse looked around, he saw nothing. *It must be my imagination. It has to be.*

Then a blur of blue and brown as someone popped out from the boulder in front of him. "Welcome!"

Jesse jumped back in alarm, until he realized it was only Parvel, grinning like a fool. "Are you trying to terrify me?" Jesse snapped.

Another grin. "Not necessarily. Just glad to see you." Parvel nodded at Anise. "I take it you had a change of heart."

"Perhaps."

"And what if she hadn't?" Jesse continued. "You would have just given yourself away."

"You were walking behind her with a sword," Parvel pointed out. "There was a good chance she meant you no harm."

"Oh."

All of a sudden, Parvel's grin faded. "Where's Silas?"

"I don't know," Jesse answered honestly. "He ran farther into the tunnels." He would tell Parvel the full story later. Then Jesse thought of something else. "Where's Rae?"

Parvel nodded to the hole in the rock by his feet.

Alarm rushed through Jesse. "She *fell?*"

"Of course not," Parvel said, laughing. "She blew out the torch and climbed down. An excellent hiding place, to be sure. I just did not have the courage to follow."

Sure enough, when Jesse peered into the pit, he saw Rae's pale arm grab onto a tiny handhold in the rock. She pulled her head up. "Nice of you to finally join us," she grunted, taking another step up. Parvel reached down to help her to her feet.

At first, she looked startled to see Anise, but, glancing at Jesse and Parvel for reassurance, she asked no questions.

"Why did you stay here?" Jesse demanded. "I thought the plan was to meet you at the surface."

Parvel shrugged his huge shoulders. "We ran into some difficulties following the map."

"What he means is, we got lost," Rae added. "Found ourselves at a dead end. We had no other choice but to hide while we came up with a plan."

"And, thankfully, you found us before the Rebellion," Parvel said. He turned to Anise, who stood there quietly, examining them in the torchlight. "Anise, isn't it?" he asked. She nodded. "Pleased to meet you. I wish it could be under different circumstances." He paused, listening for anyone approaching.

Anise was doing the same. "We must go," she urged them.

"What about Silas?" Jesse asked.

Anise didn't answer. Instead, she led the way deeper into the tunnels, and Jesse followed, although he still felt guilty leaving Silas. "He memorized the map," Rae reassured him. "He'll find his way out."

That made Jesse feel a little better, but not much. After all, if Parvel could get lost, so could Silas.

"Where are we going?" Rae asked.

"The East Escape," Anise replied. She didn't turn around. "We must be careful. A sentry may already be posted at the Escape. I am not the only one who knows it is the only way out."

They walked through another archway marked with a well, Jesse noticed, and into a smaller tunnel, one they had to stoop to get through. Still, Anise pressed on, moving faster now. Jesse found it hard to keep her pace.

Suddenly, Anise stopped. Jesse almost bumped into her. She stared into the dark, tense and rigid. "They're coming this way," she said without emotion.

Jesse could only hear the same distant shouts they had always heard. "Are you sure?"

"Yes," Anise said firmly. She turned around, then jerked her head back to them, handing Parvel her torch. "I'll lead them away. Keep going deeper to the East Escape."

"How will we know how to get there?" Rae pointed out.

"One more archway," Jesse guessed. "Marked with a heart, one on a stone near the bottom."

The voices were louder now. Anise nodded and kept backing away. "It leads to the surface. Don't trust the bridge."

With that, Anise ran into the darkness.

Parvel and Rae began to hurry even more. "She wasn't much help," Rae muttered. "What did she mean, anyway, about a bridge? She didn't even stay to explain."

"She had to go," Jesse said. "If the other Rebellion members found her helping us, who knows what could happen to her?"

The tunnel narrowed even farther at the end, with several archways on either side of the tunnel. "The heart," Parvel said, pointing to a stone near the bottom of one of them.

When they stepped through, they found themselves in a cave with a slightly higher ceiling than the tunnels. Like the caverns in the headquarters entrance, two archways were set into the stone walls. This time, though, they were not next to each other. They were on opposite sides of the long cavern, perhaps twenty paces apart.

Parvel moved cautiously forward, holding his torch out toward the stone between the two archways. There, in the same bold lettering as the riddles at the front entrance were these words:

FACE TO FACE, UPON ME GAZE,
ECHO OF WHAT YOU SEE.
AND ONLY THEN ESCAPE THIS MAZE,
REVERSED REALITY.

There was no sound in the cave for a moment as each read and re-read the rhyme. "It doesn't make sense," Rae said at last.

"Of course it doesn't *appear* to," Parvel said. "That's why it's called a riddle." He studied the words, fingering the rough stubble on his chin. "Let's take each part in turn, shall we? 'Face to face, upon me gaze.' All right, something we can see, I suppose."

"And 'escape this maze' is fairly clear," Rae added, "unless it has some hidden meaning."

"'Echo of what you see,'" Jesse muttered. "If an echo is repeated sound…."

He was beginning to get an idea, but Parvel beat him to it. "A mirror!" he pronounced, excitedly. "A reflection in a mirror is reality, only backward!" Jesse and Rae nodded. "So, how does that help us?"

"We look for the symbol of a mirror on one of the glowing stones that surround the archway," Jesse said, limping to the one on the left to examine it.

He froze halfway there, staring at the stones. Then he came closer. Finally, he leaned up to the rocks, so near that he could see the glowing white flecks that gave them their light, but his first instinct had been correct. "They're blank," he said, stunned. "There is nothing carved on any of them!"

"It's the same here," Rae called, from the right archway.

They walked slowly back to the riddle at the center. "There must be more," Jesse said, staring at the wall. But there was nothing but blank rock, flickering in the torchlight.

"Looks like the Nine got the better of us this time," Parvel said at last. "Should we just choose one?"

"And risk another trap?" Rae protested. "I'd rather go back to the other exits that Anise mentioned and face the rebels."

In the distance, Jesse thought he could hear the rebels shouting. Parvel glanced back, frowning, and said what Jesse already knew but didn't want to admit. "We're running out of time."

CHAPTER 15

If only stones could talk, Jesse thought desperately. He stared at the riddle, thinking as hard as he could. Nothing came to him.

They had solved the riddle, but what good had it done? They were still trapped. There was nothing left to do.

Except....

All right, God. I've stopped fighting. Now what?

Trust me.

So the riddle described a mirror, but there were no symbols on the rocks to indicate one. *What would a mirror's symbol be anyway?* Jesse wondered, picturing one. Then he froze. *That's it.*

"When you look into a mirror," Jesse blurted, dimly aware he was interrupting Parvel, but not caring in the least, "what do you see?"

"Yourself," Rae replied, staring at him in confusion. "Why...?"

"And is it any different than your face actually looks?"

"No," Parvel said. "Just backward—like the riddle says, 'reality reversed.' They are the same."

"Yes," Jesse said, looking significantly first at one archway, then the other. "They are the same."

Both stared at Jesse as they realized what he was saying. "You don't mean," Rae said slowly, "that these two archways lead to the same place?" Jesse nodded. "That can't be right," she said, shaking her head.

"But it has to be," Jesse insisted. "Think about it—each of the archways is a mirror of the other. That's why they have no symbols on them. Even this collection of caverns was a mirror. To get to the East Escape, we walked through archways with the same symbols as the ones at the entry—only in reverse. It's the only thing that makes sense."

"You may be right," Parvel said. "But what if that isn't the answer at all? You said that in the entrances at the front of the hideout, the wrong way was set with a terrible trap."

"We have to do something," Jesse said. "If we stay here, the rebels will catch us. This is the only way out."

Rae, and even Parvel, didn't look convinced. They both stared suspiciously at the two archways. "It's like what Parvel said earlier," Jesse added, "the hard way, choosing an archway, is the one that leads to life. The easy way, not making a choice, will kill us."

"Hmm," Parvel said, his fingers tracing the words carved into the stone. "Add to that the first letters of the riddle's lines, and I think your point is well-made, Jesse."

What? Jesse glanced back at the riddle, scanned the letters. They spelled, "FEAR."

Yes. Fear. It was what imprisoned the Roarics underground, according to Noa. It was the reason Parvel said many did not choose to do right. And it was what Jesse had struggled with since they left Mir.

But not today.

"I'll go first," Jesse said, stepping toward the passage on the right. He held out his hand to Parvel, who handed him the torch. "Once I see if it's safe, I'll call for you to follow."

Before the others could argue, Jesse limped forward, glad for once that his lame steps made his progress slow. Even with the torch, he could see nothing beyond the archway. Nothing but blackness. He stepped up to the archway, taking a deep breath.

I'm still afraid, Jesse knew, calming his shaking hand on the torch. *But I'm not choosing fear. I'm not choosing the easy way.*

With that he stepped through the archway.

After a few cautious steps, nothing happened. Jesse breathed a sigh of relief.

Then he looked up and gasped. There, to his right, was a huge wooden bridge. Unlike the bridge at his home in Mir, it was not held up by pillars, but by thick ropes attached to the ceiling above. The bridge stretched across a deep ravine, and on the other side, Jesse could see a small crack of sunlight.

"Jesse?" Rae's voice called. "Do you see anything?"

Jesse was just about to reply when two figures stepped out from the darkness at Jesse's side: Sonya holding a dagger to Silas' throat.

She faced Jesse, that familiar, cruel smile on her face. "Tell your friends to come," she whispered. "Or I kill him."

Jesse had not the least bit of doubt that she would do it. *But if I call Parvel and Rae, she'll kill us all.* "I'm looking around," he called back, in response to Rae's question.

Sonya frowned. "Tell them to come," she hissed. Silas tried to shake his head, but she held him still with her free hand, her fingernails digging into his arm. "Get both of them in here."

What do I do?

"Now, boy!"

Then a hand appeared from the darkness, wrenching the dagger out of Sonya's hand. She gasped, then toppled to the ground from an invisible blow. "Run!" a voice commanded.

It was Parvel. *What...?* It suddenly became clear to Jesse what had happened. *He trusted me enough to step through the archway on the left at the same time.*

Slowly, Jesse realized he had dropped the torch, and Silas was on the ground beside him, rolling out of the way. Parvel was struggling with Sonya, both of them a blur of motion. *She's trying to get the dagger back.*

"Jesse!" It was Rae, standing beside him. "Your sword!" He tightened his grip on it, not sure what to do. A heartbeat passed.

He handed the sword to Rae. "Take it," he shouted. "You'd do better with it than I would."

Immediately, Jesse wondered if that was a wise choice. Despite what Parvel had said about evil fighting evil, Jesse knew Rae wouldn't hesitate to stab Sonya if she thought it would save Parvel's life. *But she can't. She might strike Parvel.*

Rae appeared to realize the same thing, because all she could do was dance around the two combatants, waiting for an opportunity.

The fierce struggle for control continued, and Jesse was never able to tell who had the upper hand until Sonya, hands tightly gripping the dagger, gave Parvel a vicious kick. His body scuffed across the ground toward the bridge. Laughing in triumph, she raised the dagger high.

Jesse cried out, tried to rush forward.

But instead of plunging the dagger into Parvel's heart, she reached over to the bridge, sawing away at one of the thick ropes that held it up.

The rope snapped. Its support gone, the bridge collapsed. With a creaking groan, the boards fell into the ravine below.

Jesse stared in disbelief at the rope, still dangling loosely from the cave ceiling. *That was our way to the surface*, was all he could think.

"Do not move," Rae commanded. She was standing over Sonya, sword drawn and ready. "Drop the dagger."

Sonya did, and Parvel bent to pick it up. "It's no use," Sonya said, breathing heavily. "Even after you kill me, you can't get across. There is no escape."

So that's why she cut the rope. She would give up her own life to ensure that we are trapped here.

"Should I run her through?" Rae asked, holding her sword above Sonya's fallen form.

"No," Parvel said firmly.

Rae blew a piece of hair from her face in frustration. "I should have done it before asking. She deserves death."

"Does she?" Parvel pointed out. "Would you kill the men who are starving your family, Rae?"

Jesse knew from the instant look of hatred that she would.

"Then do not be so quick to judge Sonya for trying to take the lives of her enemies," Parvel said.

Rae just grunted, but Jesse understood. *Who knows what drove Sonya to join the Rebellion? And what about her friend, the Rebellion member Silas killed in Mir? Her bitterness is really no different than Rae's or even Silas'.* He actually began to feel sorry for her.

"Well, what do you want me to do with her?" Rae demanded. "We can't just stand here all day!"

"I think I can help with that," Silas said. He took the dagger from Parvel and walked over to the rope Sonya had cut, still dangling from the cave's ceiling. Reaching up as high as he could, he cut off a length of a few feet and threw it at Parvel. "Tie her up."

Parvel chose to use the piece to tie up Sonya's legs, using his belt for her wrists. Then he bowed to Rae. "Would you care to do the honors?" he said grandly, offering her the loose ends of the rope around Sonya's ankles.

She gave the knot a sharp pull. "There."

For good measure, Parvel took Sonya's sash, the one that had held her scabbard, and wound it around her mouth. "They will find her soon, I imagine," he said.

"As long as it's not *too* soon," Rae pointed out. "Like before we're gone."

They all stood, satisfied with their work. "So," Parvel said, "there is still the problem of getting to the other side."

Jesse glanced at the ravine. It was very wide. *And without the bridge....*

Wait. "Why did the entire structure collapse so easily?" Jesse wondered. "Sonya only cut one rope, and there were several supports. It doesn't make sense."

"You're right," Parvel agreed, peering over the edge to look at the ruins of the bridge below. "You would think that as a last escape for the rebels, the bridge would have been more stable."

"And Anise warned us not to trust the bridge," Jesse reminded them. "What if that bridge was just a trap? All of the riddles at the entrance had one. Why should this riddle be any different?"

"Riddle?" Silas asked, looking confused.

"You mean you didn't see the riddle carved into the stone by the archways?" Jesse asked in disbelief.

"No," Silas said shortly. "Sonya attacked me from behind, making me drop my sword. Then she chased me here. I had no time to look for riddles."

"You were fortunate that both archways were safe, then," Jesse said.

"But the bridge," Rae said. "Could it really have been a trap?"

Jesse nodded. "Why else would it fall apart so easily? It was probably designed that way, just like the pit you and Silas nearly fell into at the entrance."

"Hmm," Rae grunted, not sounding convinced. "Then where is the real way across? The riddle didn't say anything about that. Unless you think we should step through a mirror."

For a moment, Jesse looked blankly at Rae. "No," he muttered, staring into the darkness past her. "It's not possible."

He picked up his walking stick—he had dropped it in the chaos—and limped to his left, to the other side of the cavern.

"I hate it when he gets like this," he heard Silas mutter. Still, they followed him.

As Jesse stood on the left edge of the ravine, nothing was in front of him except blackness. *Or maybe not.*

He would look ridiculous if he were wrong, Jesse knew. But something inside of him, maybe the same voice he had heard when Roland was about to kill him, told him to try.

"May I have the Rebellion stone?" Jesse asked Silas.

He pulled back, and Jesse could see a look of distrust on his face in the dim light. "What are you going to do with it?"

Jesse groaned in frustration. *This is ridiculous.* "It's just a rock, Silas. You need to let go of it!"

Silas paused, as if shocked that Jesse would speak so sharply to him. "Besides," Jesse added, "if I'm right, you'll get it back."

Finally, Silas pulled out the stone and gave it to Jesse. Along with a tiny glimmer of daylight on the other side of the ravine, the stone's glow was the only light they had. Jesse picked up the rock and threw it into the ravine.

"What are you…?" Silas began, sounding angry. Then he just stared.

Instead of tumbling into the darkness, the stone made a sharp clicking sound, bounced a few times, and seemed to come to rest in midair. It had landed a few feet below the edge of the cliff, just out of reach.

Rae gasped. "What kind of magic is this?"

"It's not magic," Jesse insisted. "I think…I think it's a mirror. One that stretches across the canyon as a bridge."

Another pause. "That's ridiculous," Silas said. "No one builds a bridge out of a mirror. It would shatter."

"You're right," Jesse said. "Maybe it's a simple wooden bridge, overlaid with a mirror." He pointed to the Rebellion stone, still suspended in the middle of the ravine. "Look. You can see a reflection of the stone from the surface. Doesn't it make sense?"

"Not really," Rae said, but before Jesse could protest, she added, "but neither does anything else about this maze. Besides, Jesse is right. There is no other explanation."

"And it fits with the riddle," Parvel agreed.

The dim light on the other side was golden and beautiful, not the pale white of the Rebellion stones, but Jesse still could not actually see the mirrored bridge, even when he crouched down on the ground. "If only I hadn't let the torch go out," he moaned.

"Can't you touch it?" Silas asked, keeping a safe distance away from the edge.

Jesse reached down with his walking stick. For a few terrifying seconds, it cut through thin air. Then the end bumped against something invisible, but solid. "There's something there," Jesse confirmed, starting to get excited.

"But can it hold you?" Silas pointed out. "Can it hold any of us?"

"It was designed to," Parvel said, shrugging. "But we won't know for sure until we try it. I just wish we had some other choice."

Jesse smiled. "Sometimes a leap into the darkness is the only way to the light."

"Jesse, I didn't mean that literally…."

"No," Jesse interrupted. "I think you were right when you said that Parvel. Maybe you were right all along." He took a deep breath. "Let me go first."

Parvel put his hand on Jesse's shoulder. "Jesse, I can lead. You…."

"No," Jesse said, shaking his head. "I need to do this."

"Are you sure? You have no way of knowing if the bridge exists, or if it's stable. I could go first."

Jesse shook his head. "Then it wouldn't be faith."

Parvel let go, then nodded, smiling slightly. "Very good."

For a moment, Jesse stood there, clutching his walking stick and teetering on the edge of the ravine. And then he stepped out into the darkness.

After a split second of falling, his feet landed on firm ground. *So there is a bridge.* It was an eerie feeling, walking across a ravine on a mirror. He appeared to be stepping on nothing but darkness. When he reached the Rebellion stone and picked it up, he could see the dim reflection of his own legs, limping across the surface.

He could hear the others behind him, but he didn't turn to look. Instead, he focused on the light at the other end. The light that meant the surface, freedom, and the end of Riddler's Pass.

Once they reached the ledge on the other side, they stopped. Jesse almost felt afraid to go out into the open after all they had been through.

"What are we going to do now?" Rae asked in a hesitant voice. "Now that the Patrol thinks we're dead."

They all looked to Parvel. "I don't know," he said, slumping a little. Jesse looked at him closely. He looked older than his eighteen years.

Then he straightened up, and Jesse saw that familiar gleam creep back into his eyes. "But I do know I will spend the rest of my life fighting against evil and injustice, wherever it is found. Who's with me?"

"I am," Silas said. Jesse glanced at him. He didn't have the same angry expression Jesse had gotten used to over the past few days, and he didn't mention the Rebellion. *I hope that means he's left his bitterness back in the cave, where it belongs.* Somehow, Jesse wasn't entirely convinced.

"Count me in," Rae said, gripping the sword at her side.

"Rae, there are some things you cannot fight with violence alone," Parvel said mildly.

She never flinched. "I haven't found any yet."

"No," Parvel said, never looking away, "not yet."

Jesse wondered what kind of danger Parvel thought they might face in the future. Before he could ask, Parvel turned to him and asked, "And you, Jesse?"

"I'm not much of a fighter," he said, running his hand nervously along his staff.

"Don't be foolish," Rae interrupted. "You're one of us, like it or not."

It wasn't much of a compliment, except that it came from Rae. Jesse felt honored. "Then I stand with Parvel. With all of you."

Together, they stepped out of the cave. Even though the sun was setting, Jesse was nearly blinded after the near-complete darkness. Silas and Rae wasted no time in taking the lead, but Parvel stayed back, keeping pace with Jesse as he limped along.

After a few seconds, Jesse broke the silence. "I meant what I said. You were right—God is out there. And I think I want to learn more about Him, even though I don't know anything right now."

Parvel smiled. "You're well on your way just by wanting that Jesse. But I must warn you; you are taking a big risk by becoming a believer in God. We have many enemies, you know."

"What do you mean?"

"I've heard of some who have been imprisoned, driven underground, tortured, and even killed by the king's men, because of what they believe."

"So, if I decide to become a believer in God, King Selen might try to kill me," Jesse summarized, smiling a little. "Something that he's already doing."

"This is serious, Jesse."

"So am I." Jesse stood. "You have a lot to teach me, Parvel. I must admit, I paid very little attention to the teachings of the priest in Mir."

Parvel joined him, staring down the mountain road, and gave a resolute nod. "There will be time. Besides, those priests don't know the real truth about God. They talk as if faith is a dry, boring thing." He smiled, and it was like daylight breaking through after a long night. "It's the greatest true story of all time, Jesse. And you know how much I love to tell stories."

"Come on, you two!" Silas called from up ahead. "The Rebellion will catch up with all of us at your speed."

In response, Jesse and Parvel began to walk a little bit faster—but only a little bit.

"Where to begin?" Parvel wondered out loud. He paused, closing his eyes. When he spoke again, it was in the familiar, rhythmic tone used by all in District One when they told a story. "It started with darkness and emptiness. Before time was created, God was. And He spoke into the darkness and created the light...."

And even though the sun was sinking in the sky, Jesse didn't wish daylight would last longer. He wasn't afraid of the darkness because this time he was not alone.

Somehow, he knew he would never be alone again.

CHAPTER 16

The Patrol was growing restless. Demetri knew it was true, even though none of them had dared complain to his face. He noticed it in the mutters during the night watches, in the way the men ate their dwindling rations in silence.

"Guarding a pile of rocks," he had heard one of them say. And it was true; the Deep Mines showed no sign of the Youth Guard, no sign of life at all.

Silent as a tomb.

A few of the Patrol members who had left Mir with Demetri would never return. Two had been crushed in the cave-in that had collapsed the tunnel. Demetri himself had barely gotten out in time. Once the shaking and rumbling stopped, he sent sentries back in to investigate. Past the large main cave with the ruins in it, everything else had collapsed. The Youth Guard members were dead. They could not have survived.

At least, that was what Demetri told himself. But he had seen the three young people survive circumstances just as dangerous back in Da'armos.

That was why he had waited so long, sent out groups of Patrol to check the perimeter, and made sure there were no signs of life. Even if, by some miracle, the three had survived the cave-in, they would be trapped. Nearly three full days had passed. Three days without food or water.

Demetri grimaced. It was a hard way to die.

But I had no choice, he told himself. *Aleric and the others would have killed my brother if I had refused this mission.*

Aleric had reminded him of this in his last vision the night before. That's how Demetri was sure the three were dead. "I do not see them at all now," Aleric told him. "Not even brief glimpses. I have not been able to for nearly two days now. They have fallen."

Reaching into his cloak, Aleric had pulled out the dragon medallion, decorated with Demetri's family crest. "Report to the governor's palace in District Two. A man named Chancellor Doran will record the death of the three in the Book. He will give your crest back to you to replace your Guard medallion. You have done your duty."

Again, Demetri felt the burning medallion against his chest. It was almost a familiar, warming sensation by now. His hand went to it.

"That is," Aleric added, "unless you wish to join us for life."

For life...or for death. He would have to kill more Youth Guard. Demetri was sure of that. Every five years, he would be sent out with the other Guard Riders.

There would be danger involved in the missions. After years in the desert, the idea had a strange appeal for Demetri.

He enjoyed traveling, and he appreciated facing opponents more clever than petty thieves and pickpockets.

And there was the matter of the medallion. The nightmares were starting to seem more like visions that gave him power and knowledge. Demetri wasn't sure he wanted to give that up. He reached into his shirt and traced the *A* inside the broken circle, the emblem of the king.

"I will think on it," was all he said.

When he woke up, his determination to join the Guard Riders had faded. The medallion's influence seemed to die down when he was awake. He didn't feel quite as powerful or invincible. *Just sore and tired of being trapped in this mountain, like the other men.*

It was time to make the announcement to the Patrol. They could leave now that Aleric had given him permission.

To Demetri's right, two Patrol members were sitting beside the fire. Demetri glanced at them briefly, out of the corner of his eye. They were talking about him. He could tell by the looks on their faces. He had heard many rumors about who he was and why he wanted to kill three young people. Patrol members loved gossip more than a village full of old women.

Demetri did not like working with the Patrol. They were strong and good with the sword, of course, but many of them were foolish and self-serving. *Perhaps Aleric should consider using the Youth Guard to serve the king, instead of killing them all.*

Except, Demetri knew, many would refuse and fight the king to the end, if they knew his true character. *That is, after all, why they were chosen.* Yes, the Guard Riders who held the musters and chose young people for the Guard looked at their physical and mental strength, as well as other abilities. But they were also trained to notice young people with high moral standards.

Demetri chuckled to himself. *I really can't understand why I was chosen, then. They must have needed one scoundrel among the bunch.*

Demetri knew he must be a scoundrel, because he knew normal people would feel remorse after killing three innocent young people. He did not.

He stood and walked over to the Patrol members on watch duty. "It has been three days," Demetri announced. "The three Youth Guard are dead."

"Youth Guard?" one of the men said, and Demetri cursed himself inwardly for his mistake. "You said they were young Rebellion leaders."

Of course, the Patrol member believed the Youth Guard worked for the king. That is what they all believed, except for the few leaders who knew the truth—the Guard Riders.

"They were Youth Guard; then they defected to the Rebellion, after swearing an oath to serve the king—the worst kind of traitors," he lied.

No, the worst kind of traitors are those who betray their friends for their own gain.

Demetri silenced the thought and the memories that came with it. "You may all go back home to your outposts," he said. The mountain paths were clearly marked; he did not have to waste his time escorting the Patrol members back to District One.

"What about you?" one of the men asked.

"I go on," was all Demetri said.

On to Davior, the capital of District Two, to report to the chancellor, the one Aleric had told him would record the death of the three.

Perhaps I can convince him to let me see this Book, Demetri decided. *It would give me great pleasure to strike out their names myself.*

He glanced back at the mountain one last time. There was an old saying in the desert, which, when translated into Amarian, said, "Even the rocks cry out for justice." *Was justice done here? Did the Youth Guard members deserve to die?*

It doesn't matter, Demetri decided, turning away. He reached for the medallion again, and the way the metal cut into his tight fist made him feel strong and powerful again. *Justice is dead. And so are the Youth Guard.*